The Eye that Watches the Sparrow

ODESSA DRAYTON-ITON

DRAYTON-ITON COMMUNICATIONS, DBA

For more information about this title, please contact:

Odessa Drayton-Iton
Drayton-Iton Communications, dba
Odessaiton@aol.com

The Eye That Watches The Sparrow

By Odessa Drayton-Iton

ISBN-13: 978-0615868523
ISBN-10: 0615868525

"The LORD is near to those who have a broken heart and saves those who are crushed in spirit." -- *Psalm 34:18*

"If at first you don't succeed…
Cry! … then try again."
-- Deirdre Parks

The crack of dawn quietly eases up and over a hill that nestles a row of tranquil carriage houses and small colonials on a chilly spring morning. The municipal sanitation truck halts in front of each house and gobbles up the identical blue plastic trash bins one-by-one.

"Haul!" a tall muscular man shouted over the loud grind of the trash cylinder as he jumped onto the back of the slow moving vehicle clinging to the sidebar till the next shortstop. It was a new assignment dispatched to Charles Monroe and his crew after the last Christmas holiday season. A couple of the older guys complained of the steep inclines and number of houses that needed to be served on the south end of town and shrewdly suggested that the younger guys in the garage switch with the more seasoned but weary veterans. As crew leader, he felt compassion for the older workers and agreed to the switching of assignments.

As Charles mounted the truck for the last set of houses ahead he noticed a woman rushing out of her house and toward the car now being partially blocked by his garbage truck. It was hard not to notice the tall statuesque woman in the fitted business suit and heels. Already close to six-feet, the extra 2 inches made her look like an Amazon off to battle. In perpetual motion, carrying multiple bags and other random paraphernalia, she looked like a one-woman show. Out of habit, the woman quickly looked both ways and scurried across the small tree lined street, dodging successfully around the back end of the departing truck to her waiting car. Although the baseball mitt, Frisbee and an empty fast-food supersize soda cup in the back seat of her car were evidence of at least one teenager attached to the attractive woman who looked to Charles to be in her late 30's, she was leaving her house by herself this morning. Rushing out to face the world at the crack of dawn, alone. Deirdre never noticed the gentleman picking up her trash, or noticing her, at all.

"Whatcha' looking at Son?" Quips Ty.

"Man don't even waste your time looking at that. You're already a garbage man. You don' t need the extra baggage that one is obviously carrying."

He continues, "She's too old for you anyhow, Son."

"You know you need to learn to mind your business, Negro. She's 40 tops, no more," says Charles in his own defense.

"Nah Son, that sistah's about to hit 50 sooner rather than later. Let me give you some more lessons on women again, Son; since you don't seem to be catching on to nothing but them history books that you read all the time." Teases Ty. "Listen to the teacher, professor, and learn!" he emphatically continues.

"If you want to know how old a woman is look at two things. Her eyes and the set of her mouth when she thinks no one is looking. Them eyes and that mouth! Son, that'll tell it all. Ya see, sooner or later all them emotions and changes women be going through and taking a brotha' through starts to show up on their faces, man. I'm tellin' you man, that stuff hides all up in their eyes and around the corners of their mouths. Believe me man, I ain't lyin! Ain't no MAX Cosmetics, Cover Gal or Cover Boy gonna cover-up 30 or 40 years of bitterness," finishes Ty self-satisfied.

"Man, you don't know that woman. How do you know that she is bitter?" demands Charles.

"BW Radar, man!"

"What?"

"It's my Bitter Woman Radar, brother. I can sense a bitter sister a thousand miles away. Just something in their way about themselves. They don't have to say a word. I know when Joe done 'em wrong and they mad at life and every breathin' brother on God's green earth!"

Charles had enough experience with women to know that everything that Ty was saying wasn't a lie. However, he had learned over the years in and out of love and various dalliances that there was always something precious and of tremendous value in the heart of a woman once you cut through the outer defenses.

"Love is not selfish…" --Grandpop Matthew Monroe

Charles, a 38 year old sanitation worker and college drop-out left school a year before graduating to help his ailing mother. It was Charles' dream to attend Heritage College. When he learned of his acceptance he knew that God had answered his prayers. As a young child, he was a bright but rambunctious boy who always had his head in a book and a rock or stick of some sort in his hand. His early entrance to a prestigious college at the tender age of 16 was actually of no surprise but great relief to just about everyone in the neighborhood who had to replace many a broken window over his childhood years because of his ceaseless rock throwing.

The fact that he never knew his biological father seemed to add fuel to his determination to succeed in life by the time he approached his teens. However, the same impetus as a grade schooler kept him in just enough mischief to keep his grandfather, uncles and mother on his case.

His mother Ernestine Banks, his Grandpop Matthew and Mamma Jo, their tightly knit church family, his baseball and basketball coaches and "Uncle Pete" helped make it happen for a young black boy who despite his raw intellectual brilliance was statistically destined to be relegated to the bottom.

Against the odds, his hard work and diligence paid off, he was finally living his dream of being a Heritage Man like Uncle Pete. Then seemingly without warning, the late night calls began to come with greater frequency as his mother began a long battle with breast cancer that eventually took her life. Devastated, Charles, an only child to his single mom dropped out of college late in the second semester of his junior year and returned to New Jersey to care for his dying mother.

1989, Spring Semester, Heritage College, Atlanta, GA

"It's for you. Sounds serious," his roommate Rick says offering him a black phone receiver with a mismatched off-white and tangled cord that made it difficult for him to properly place it on his ear in a reclining position. Wincing at the digital alarm clock noting the wee hour, he quickly sat up on the dorm bed and adjusted the aberrant phone piece.

"Uncle Pete?" Charles inquired.

"Son, you need to come home as soon as you can." The voice on the other end informed.

"Your mother isn't doing well," finished the gentleman who had been a father figure and mentor to the scholarly young college student most of his life.

"Yes, sir." Charles responded as the older gentleman on the other end of the phone continued to give instructions and encouragement. Placing the phone down slowly on its hook while attempting to take in all that he heard, the stunned young man suddenly uttered,

"Wow. My mom is dying". His sad announcement seemed to be directed to no one in particular even though his roommate of the past 3 years, sat upright in the twin bed directly across from his watching his face intently.

"Man, cancer doesn't have to be a death sentence. Modern medicine has saved a lot of people. Don't give up, Man. Your mom is strong, she can beat this." Rick encouraged.

"Yeah, Man. I know. Thanks."

"Look, I've got to pack-up and get back to Jersey this weekend. Can you let my professors know that I had to leave because of a family emergency? I'll mail-in my unfinished papers and finals before the end of the semester." Charles finished.

"Sure, Man. Anything. You know that you're my main man." Rick stated emphatically. Awkwardly rising from his bed he gives Charles a hand pound. His usually clear bright eyes now shadowed with sadness.

"Whatever you need. I got your back, brother." Rick affirms.

The Present...

Although Charles made a deathbed promise to his mother to return to school and finish his degree... it was a dream deferred. Twenty years later he found himself picking up the garbage of the well-to-do of Northern New Jersey, convinced that it is only one degree of separation that removed him from the intellectual and social circles of those whom he served. The educated served by the less educated; the proverbial haves v. the have nots... or have not as much. Two decades with the Sanitation Department was an education that he could not have paid for at any university.

However, his yearning to learn did not die with the evaporating years, nor did his promise to his mom. Although he did not take up the pursuit of finishing his degree until a decade ago, he always managed to take a class here and there. Sometimes he'd pile on as many classes as he could bear while working full-time and overtime at the Sanitation Department. Other times he would let as many as 2 years lapse without cracking a college catalog.

Nevertheless, it all eventually added up and a decade later he was just 9 credits shy of his coveted bachelors degree with a double major in History and English.

"Better late, than never," Charles whispered to himself as a means of self-encouragement as he puts the finishing touches on his 17th Century English Lit paper. He chuckled to himself as he stared at the laptop screen watching his huge file compress into a zippered document that he would in an instant e-mail to his invisible professor. To think that he was about to earn 3 more credits toward his degree and he hadn't stepped foot on a college campus in over a decade. He was thankful for the technology that was helping him to redeem the time.

Ironically, it was in moments like this, alone on his laptop in the wee hours of the morning that he most often felt regret for the lost years. Charles looked around the relatively comfortable and well-furnished room that he sat in with only the blue light of the laptop screen bouncing back on his face and remembered that all was not lost in the passing years that seemed to come and go like a vapor. His finances were secure, he owned his home and drove a car that he wasn't ashamed to be seen in as a man in his late 30's.

He often mused to himself how so many do not seem aware of or appreciate the privilege of getting a good education or going to college. Not that he didn't already know it—but now he truly appreciated the oft repeated United Negro College Fund slogan: "*A mind is a terrible thing to waste.*" Yes, starting and more importantly finishing a college degree was a privilege not to be taken for granted.

Ever ambitious and resourceful with a deep and abiding faith, Charles vowed again to himself and to his God that he would 'hang in there' with the hope of finishing his unfinished business even if it meant being an almost 40 year old man spending many late nights on an old laptop taking a couple of on-line courses at a time.

"Despise not the small things (beginnings)…"

– A favorite Proverb of Charles Monroe

*"Sometimes we miss God's simple blessings
because we're so preoccupied with the cares of the world."*
--Maggie Moore

Charles didn't notice much around him as he stood in line to pay for the new usb thumb drive that he needed to finish his History paper. One paper down, one to go as he inched toward the finish line to his bachelors degree one class or two at a time. He was more than a little bleary eyed from the late night rendezvous with his trusty laptop. The last 9 credits were killing him. What was he thinking? A double major at 38 years old with a full-time job and other commitments? Had he forgotten that he was 16 when he made that brilliant decision? So why was a 38 year old man following the plan of a 16 year old boy with stars in his eyes for his bright future more than two decades ago? Did he really need the degree? His job with the Sanitation Department was secure despite recent municipal layoffs, he owned his home, his bills were paid and he carried only mortgage debt.

"$22.50, sir." States the cashier interrupting Charles thoughts.

"Oh, here ya'go," he says handing over his gold bank debit card with the charge card logo. Grandpop Matthew, his mother's father, taught him to always pay cash and if he couldn't pay cash for something, he couldn't afford it. He recalled hearing stories of how

Gramps and his four brothers had a fresh fruit and fish stand down South in the 1930's right after the Depression. Their business thrived in a small South Carolina community from 1939 until World War II began in 1941. Two of the five Monroe brothers enlisted in the army and waited anxiously to be shipped off to Germany which seemed to take forever for so many Black soldiers due to segregation and flat out racists military policies and practices that prevailed at the time. Many African American soldiers never saw any action during World War II despite their passionate desire to defend their country.

However, both of Charles' great uncles finally got their aching desire fulfilled to defend the sovereignty of America's shores of freedom in both Germany and France. Gramps and the two youngest Monroe brothers remained behind and ran a successful small business "cash only" that eventually allowed Gramps and his brothers that wanted to leave the South in the late 40's to relocate their young families to Northern New Jersey with seed money to open a small corner store in their new northern neighborhood.

Not having a dad around as a boy was admittedly tough, but God seemed to compensate in a lot of ways with strong fatherly figures in Charles' young life like Uncle Pete, Grandpop Matthews and his Great Uncles. So why didn't the hunger for a daddy ever go away?

"Thank you for shopping E-zone, sir. Have a nice day," chirps the high school student behind the cash register.

"Thanks, you too," automatically replies Charles as he stuffs his card back into his wallet, grabs his bag and leaves. Checking his cell phone for the time, he heads in the direction of the mall's Food Court just beyond the store entrance. Charles queues up in line behind a woman and her teenage son and patiently waits for his turn to be served.

"Look Tommy, I'm really tired and want to go home. Can you please make up your mind? What's it going to be? Pizza or a burger?" implores the obviously exasperated mother of the teenager who looked to be around 13 years old.

"Can I have fries with it?"

"With what? The pizza or the burger, Tommy?"

"The Pizza." The boy states resolutely.

"That's what I thought you meant. No, boy you're not going to eat fries with pizza! Burger and fries or pizza. That's it!" Declares the mom adding, "Now order or you won't eat at all because I'm not cooking tonight!" Charles couldn't help but chuckle to himself and crack a small smile as he allowed the banter between mother and son to interrupt his preoccupation with all that he had to do in the next two days.

"Your pizza will take about 3 minutes , Mam."

"Thank you," says the mother of the teen looking relieved to have the transaction settled. Stepping aside so that Charles can place his order , the woman digs through her over-stuffed pocketbook in search of her wallet. While digging her cell phone blast a pretty classical melody. Exasperated again, the woman silences the phone and continues the search for her wallet.

"PhillyCheese Steak with everything on it, man." States Charles as he quickly produces a twenty dollar bill and hands it to the smaller man behind the counter.

"And put this little brother's pizza on my tab." Adds Charles in a random act of kindness.

"Oh, that's really sweet of you, but you don't have to do that." Says the mom producing her own ten dollar bill to pay for her son's order.

"No Mam, please, I need a blessing," Charles half-seriously jokes.

"Well I don't want to get in the way of God blessing you! Thanks that's very kind of you."

"Say thank you, Tommy," demands the mother.

"Thanks." Tommy parrots without looking directly at Charles.

"You're pretty tall, Man. Play ball?"

"Yes." Tommy says looking up and meeting Charles' eyes.

"Here you are, Mam," the counter man returns interrupting the friendly exchange handing a piping hot personal pizza to the woman.

"Thanks, again!" says the mother as she passes the hot food to her son and returns both her cash and wallet to her pocketbook.

"No problem," says Charles reaching for his order that comes immediately after the boy's pizza. Something in the back and forth between the mother and son reminded him of his relationship with his own single-mom as a teen. Perhaps it was presumptuous to think that the woman wasn't married, but it was the lens through which Charles saw most mothers and sons when there wasn't a man physically present. Besides, she had "that look" as his buddy Ty would say.

"Tommy, be careful with that. It's extremely hot."
Warns the woman walking just a few steps ahead of the boy toward the mall's exit.

"Yeees, mom." The boy drones while playfully bouncing the hot pizza box slightly in the air. Heading in the opposite direction, Charles exits the eatery fully focused on his meal. Taking a huge bite of the savory hot sandwich he moans,

"Umph!" to himself. "That's good!" as he slowly walks toward the mall exit and out to his car contently chomping on his sandwich.

"Stolen water is always sweet…" --Grandma Mae

Deirdre unloaded the groceries from the trunk of the car hoping that the perishables were ok. The stop at the mall to get Tommy a much needed pair of sneakers took about an hour longer than she had planned and ran into her dinner prep time. So much for the peppered-steak that she was hankering for . Tommy would have to be content with his pizza and she with whatever she could find already prepared in the frig.

"Tommy please take your pizza inside and comeback and help me with these groceries." Deirdre calmly instructs wearied from running evening errands following a challenging day at work.

"Oh man, do I have to? I'm hungry!" The teenager complains.

"Boy, I know one thing, you better get your behind in the house, put the pizza down on the kitchen table and get back out here and help me with these bags or you won't see your game system again until next summer!" Deirdre threatens knowing that she is exaggerating to make a point in attempt to gain control over a constantly volatile situation.

"Ah, man. I always have to do everything around here all the time! What am I, a slave?" the teen grumbles while stomping into the house leaving his pizza on the hood of the car.

"Tommy!!!" Deirdre now at her wits end.

"Why don't you listen, boy? I said to take the pizza inside first, and then come and get the groceries!"

"Whew! Lord please help me with this child!" she says exasperated for the umpteenth time of the evening. "If you just give me strength, I'll make it," she continues while walking into the two-family house where she rents a small but inviting upstairs apartment.

The evening fast forwards to a close as Deirdre rinses the soap off of the last dish in the sink. How so many dishes accumulated even when she didn't cook a full meal was a mystery to her. Dishes had a way of growing out of her sink when left unguarded; a lot like old thoughts and memories. Tonight she felt every second of her 48 years. It was a feeling that she struggled with that seemed to surface more than usual in the past year or so. She always looked and felt a lot younger than she was until recently. Perhaps it was just the loneliness. Or was it anger and silent frustration catching up with her?

She still wasn't where she needed to be financially although she had come a long way since the layoff 6 years ago. Who would have thought that it would take so long to recover from a job loss and transition into a new career?

Nevertheless, her biggest challenge of late seemed to no longer be financial, but relational. The one thing that she believed that she could do right was be a mother to her son. Although, she never planned to do it as a single parent. Divorce was never in her vocabulary…or in her heart but somehow it forced its way into her life causing more emotional devastation than she could have ever imagined. Tommy was rebelling against her parental authority after years of bouncing between two households and led to believe from an early age by his doting father that his mother was the cause of their family break-up. What an absolute lie.

She's was brokenhearted, busted and disgusted.

How could she raise her son to forgive and love unconditionally when she harbored her own deeply rooted resentments and disappoints in love and in life? How did she arrive at such a place?

Deirdre and Phil Michaels met at a mutual friend's 4th of July cookout about 15 years ago. The two talkative and attractive urbane professionals hit it off immediately. It was literally, love at first sight! 3 years of living together proceeded a short engagement and a 7 year marriage.

Little Tommy was conceived on their honeymoon night and was in grade school when Phil unceremoniously announced his intentions to end their 10 year relationship to wed his colleague, Michelle Ross. Michelle was the only female on Phil's team and his direct report. She surreptitiously became a close confidant over the years with her role as *"office wife"* beginning as an innocuous private joke between the New Technologies Director and the ambitious Project Manager. Her constant presence and available ear and shoulder to lean on gave Phil a sounding board that he didn't know he craved.

It was all business at first… the long strategy meetings, friendly afternoon chats in his office or her cubicle that naturally grew more personal in nature. Slowly but surely, Phil began to bring his personal pain, work pressures and even his marital woes to Michelle over lunch, an after work drink or two, a late evening project wrap up.

Seemingly innocent walks by her workspace on the way to the employee lounge to grab a cup of coffee gave them multiple opportunities to share a laugh, a work related anecdote or musing about a fellow co-worker. To go on endlessly about something silly that they both happened to see on television the night before, became a familiar routine between the two.

With each passing encounter, the topic of discussion began to matter less. Any excuse to be in each others presence would do. Satisfying the growing attraction that was obviously becoming more than professional was all that mattered to either of them. Eventually closed door meetings and the necessity of frequent business travel became commonplace. Likewise, the obvious lingering that they indiscreetly did in offices and conference rooms after the close of daily meetings with the unsolicited excuse of needing to go over details that did not warrant further attention; predictably raised eyebrows and provided fodder for the office rumor mill.

Phil had the pain, Michelle always had the balm. How could he not fall in love with her, despite the fact that he was a married man and father? Who wouldn't? A man has needs and has to do whatever is necessary to make and keep himself happy. After all, life is too short to spend it being miserable.

Working lunches eventually became early evening dinners together without his wife or her fiancé. It took only a precious few unexpected out-of-town business meetings that required their team efforts to lead to an affair that caught no one at the office by surprise.

Phil, a married man with a young child; Michelle engaged to a college sweetheart felt themselves destined for each other despite their ties to significant others. No one understood or knew how deep and right their love for each other was and never would. Everyone said that it was wrong, but they knew like no one else that it was right. It was them against the world.

Leaning against the customized center island in the fairly contemporary kitchen of their idyllic suburban home, Phil without flinching looked Deirdre straight in the eye and announced,

"I simply am no longer happy with our relationship. In fact, it makes me very unhappy. Michelle is frankly everything that I've ever wanted in a woman. She supports me in everyway and I really need that."

"Supports you in everyway?" Deirdre asked not believing what her ears were clearly hearing. "Phil I carried you financially, emotionally, sexually and every other way through grad school!!!" exclaimed Deirdre feeling herself begin to fall apart.

"You wouldn't have an MBA or even your current position if it weren't for my supporting YOU!" she finally screamed hurt and confused.

"Whatever, Deirdre." Phil dismissively responded.

"The bottom line is that I am no longer in love with you and don't see any need to continue our marriage."

"What about our son, Phil? What about Tommy?" Deirdre questioned wounded and waiting Phil's response.

"I have every intention of maintaining a healthy relationship with my son. This is not about Tommy, this is about us, Deirdre. Our marriage doesn't work. We are no longer compatible. We haven't slept together in ages. We don't even find each other attractive anymore. Our differences are irreconcilable."

"Mom you didn't read the Bible to me yet," Tommy yells groggily from his bedroom snapping Deirdre out of her reverie back into the present.

"I'll be there in a moment, Tommy." Deirdre responds while removing the trash bag from the cabinet underneath the sink that is now free of dirty dishes. Shaking the debris from the silver drainer into the bag, she knots it and sets it aside to go out on the curb tonight before she retires. She rarely had time to do anything in the morning that wasn't directly connected to getting her and Tommy out of the house in a timely fashion. On those rare mornings when she did get out of the house super early the sanitation truck was already on the block making its weekly rounds. Sometimes she poked around a little longer inside to avoid going out while the garbage truck was in front of the house to avoid seeing and smelling garbage first thing in the morning.

Rinsing her hands and drying them on a cotton towel on the counter beside her, she leaves the kitchen and in a few brief steps is in Tommy's room. Settling down on the ottoman that she moved out of the living room into his bedroom, she picks up his Youth Bible and proceeds.

"He that dwells in the secret place of the Most High shall abide under the shadow of the Almighty. I will say of the Lord, He is my refuge and my fortress; My God, in Him I will trust." Reads Deirdre noticing Tommy's sleep heavy eye-lids.

"Tommy, did you hear anything that I just read?" Deirdre asks her drowsy son.

"Yeah, most of it. Good night, mom," the teenager bids.

"Good night, son." Deirdre says, lightly placing a kiss on his forehead without risk of rebuff due to his instant submission to heavy snoring.

"Son, it doesn't matter where you start in life; it matters most how you finish and the type of man you become in the process."
-- Uncle Pete

8 year old Charles is in the Principal's office explaining how he accidentally set off the fire alarm during the school assembly when another alarm mysteriously goes off in the hallway...

It's 4am and his screen was frozen on the *"Your file has been sent"* message. Groaning he shut down the laptop and the repeated bleep of his cell phone alarm that worked its way into his dreams and headed for the shower. Once out the door the fog that held his head captive in the wee hours began to clear enough for him to notice the pristine morning sky. It was the crack of dawn when bright orange co-mingles with the soft lavender in the morning twilight above. Charles breathed deeply taking it all in, exhaled and pulled out of his driveway.

"Miss Maggie, How ya' doing this morning?"

"Just fine, baby. How are you?"

"Good. And gonna be a whole lot better come 4 o' clock." Charles declares pushing his timecard through the clock mechanism and dropping it quickly back into its slot.

"I hear ya. How's your schooling coming along? You should be just about finished, aren't ya?"

" Yep. Just turned in my last two papers for this semester last night. Three down, six to go!"

"Six classes?" the older woman asks amazed.

"No, actually I have only about two or three classes left to take which is about 6 credit hours depending on the classes. I am almost home, Miss Maggie!" Charles cheers arms raised above his head.

"That's good son, I'm so proud of you. Now when ya' gonna' let me introduce you to my grand-daughter? You're the type of young man she needs to be with, not them fellas she brings around the house. Why a girl with as much going for herself as Desiree has got going for herself would choose these boys out here with nothing going on? Livin' all up in their mamma's and grandmamma's houses doing nothing. Pretty girl. Finished community college and everything. You'd make a nice boyfriend for her. See here's a picture we took last week at her mother's 50th Birthday party. Ain't she pretty?"

"Yes, Mam. She's very pretty," Charles complies looking over Miss Maggie's shoulder at the photo of a 20-ish young woman bearing a remarkable resemblance to her grandmother.

"…and I see where she gets her good looks from!"

"Oh boy, go on now!" Miss Maggie blushes shooing Charles away. Charles laughs and gives the older woman a shoulder hug and walks away smiling and whistling a catchy tune down the long corridor to the truck dispatch area of the garage.

Popping his head in the locker room he notices a pink message slip with his name on it posted on the crew bulletin board. Without stepping fully into the empty room he snatches the message off the board and keeps moving toward the truck dispatch area for his 10 minute crew meeting before leaving the garage.

Walking and reading he bids a fellow co-worker good morning without breaking his gait. Whipping out his cell phone like a gun in a holster, he flips it and pushes one button that speed dials Uncle Pete.

"Good Morning, Uncle Pete, I see that you called me yesterday right after I left the garage. How are you?"

"Fine, son. How are you?"

"Good, Uncle Pete. Just finished those History and English Lit papers at 2 am this morning. I'm dog tired, but happy as a pig in mud!"

"I hear ya', son." Uncle Pete chuckles.

"I'm really proud of you," the older gentleman offers with fatherly pride. He continues, "Just wanted to schedule our monthly meeting time for this week since I had to go out of town last month and will be traveling again next week to Washington, DC for an NAACP awards dinner."

"What honor are you getting this time? I don't know anyone who gets as many honors and awards as you do!" says Charles proudly with happiness for his mentor.

"Oh son, it's not that I am so special, I'm just one of the few early Civil Rights activists that fought on the frontlines still around to talk about it. The old guard is dying off and it's our duty to keep telling the story and make sure that it is heard and understood by the next generation. Soon we'll all be gone onto glory, and only you and your children will be here to tell our story."

"Well, I'll be here to tell it. Don't know about any children. Kind of need a wife with that order, Unc."

"Well, what ya' doing about it , son?"

"Not much, I guess."

"This sounds like a Saturday conversation, son. Why don't you get on to your work and we'll talk when we meet this week. The diner at 3pm Saturday afternoon?"

"Sounds good, Uncle Pete. Looking forward to seeing you." Charles flips his phone close and continues across the garage to the waiting crew and truck.

Uncle Pete was the longtime "friend" of Ernestine Banks, Charles' mother. Pete was the closest thing to a father Charles had ever known. Pete never married his mother, but cared deeply for both her and Charles. He often took the inquisitive and energetic little boy to ballgames, tennis matches, the racetrack. Uncle Pete felt it his duty to show up and support young Charles in just about every major event in his life. The help that he gave him with his scholarship application to Heritage College of which he was an alumni; was instrumental to his gaining acceptance to the college.

Pete also helped as much as he could when Charles' mom took ill. Pete eventually married a woman 20 years his junior and by the time Charles was in his 3rd year at Heritage had two small children with his young wife. Despite the obvious responsibilities of the elder gentleman, he remained faithful to his friendship and love for Charles and his mom. Pete was with Charles at his mom's bedside when she drew her last breath of earthly life. Pete also helped Charles land his current job at the Sanitation Department in town when he left Heritage to care for his mother 20 years ago.

The Sanitation Department had been good to Charles, just as it had been for Uncle Pete when he was a big strapping teenage boy growing up in the segregated South of the 1950's. Uncle Pete began working at the Montgomery County Sanitation Department as a teenager during the hot Alabama summers.

He was 17 the first summer that he was allowed to actually go out on the truck and make the rounds in the neighboring Claybourne County that shared municipal services with Montgomery. He had worked inside doing janitorial work for two previous summers. The chance to go out with the men and pick up the refuse of the local community was a promotion in his estimation. Working next to the more experienced sanitation crew members, sharing jibes and stories as they inched from house to house relieving their neighbors of their life debris and trash.

The summer of '56 would also be his last summer with the Department before going off to Heritage College to study Political Science and Religion. The next summer would find him on the prestigious Atlanta campus in the early admissions summer prep program for incoming freshman. Not bad for a second-generation Heritage man, sanitation worker and grandson of an Alabama sharecropper.

It was a normal Alabama morning. Pete jumped off the moving truck to retrieve the garbage can in front of Mrs. Morley's enormous antebellum Victorian that most would consider a mansion. The Morley Plantation was a historic landmark in Montgomery. It's main house still stood stately commanding both awe and admiration. Pink and white camellias, lavender azaleas and orange daylilies seductively wrapped themselves around the peripheral of the veranda allowing the eye to capture just a glimpse of the structure that was once slave quarters just beyond the white billow of dogwood trees behind the main house.

Pete was an earnest teen, who despite the constrictions of a segregated southern society; showed genuine proper respect for his elders whether black or white. The respect that he demonstrated toward the white members of his community was not under compulsion, for he believed that all human beings regardless of race or color deserved respect. The fact that segregation demanded his submission to Montgomery's white citizens was of no personal consequence for Pete. His core value system was ingrained by way of familial discipline and training despite how he and other people of color were treated by most of the white members of his small southern town.

He heard the heart-shaped locket hit the ground before he saw it. Stooping low to pick up the lost piece of jewelry extending his long muscular arms and his broad well-developed shoulders that were manly beyond that of his tender 17 years. Summers of helping his father and uncles plow, plant and harvest their family's back 40 acres with ole' Juke the stubborn mule; made the boy a manchild.

Wiping away beads of sweat that now congregated directly over his left brow, with the rescued locket securely in hand, the young Pete stealthily moved toward the large mahogany double doors. He proceeded to grasp the large brass knocker when Mrs. Morley suddenly appeared like an apparition half clad in a negligee that revealed far more than the 17 year old Negro boy needed to see of a white woman in the 1950's South. Although Pete's body blocked any view of the woman from the street, Pete had an eye full of the Lady of the House who positioned herself slightly in front of the huge door.

"Oh, you're such a doll for finding my locket," Mrs. Morley crooned.

"I was about to lose my natural head over the loss of my precious heirloom," she said lightly adjusting a soft silky layer of her sheer nightgown as she reached for the locket. "A gift passed down from my great- great grandmother Fanny Louise Palmer in the late 1800's, of course." Mrs. Morley continued without care or concern for the shock that registered on the young man's face.

Pete stood still with his arm stiffly stretched out in front of him with the jewel dangling from his index finger. He had never seen a naked woman of any race, creed or color...and the full alabaster figure in front of him sent strange sensations shooting through his body. His first impulse was to take flight because his head began to throb as his mind shouted,

"Trouble!!!!" but for some reason his feet would not obey and he remained stuck in the cement that had suddenly risen from the ground and fermented around his work boots.

"Run!!!" the voice in his head shouted again. But, again his legs would not budge from the spot that they were in and he found himself walking into the mansion at the older woman's beck and call.

"Pete!" a frantic but familiar voice came sailing behind his back as he stepped into the foyer of the large home that seemed to have as many exotic southern flowers on display inside as outdoors. Jake burst through the unlocked heavy doors like a hurricane.

"Mornin' Mizzuz Morley!" he shouted loud enough for help to come out of the woodworks. He needed eye and ear witnesses and got them instantaneously. The older man breathed a sigh of relief as at least a half dozen servants immediately appeared in the foyer of the great house with looks of confusion and concern.

"Oh, how are you, Jake?" responded Mrs. Morley with the innocence of a child.

"Fine morning we're having," she offered continuing her demeanor of virtue despite her half clad body before a small crowd of Negro servants and two garbage men.

"Yes, Mam, it is indeed." Jake responded without lifting his eyes from the safety of the floor.

"I saw the boy follow you in the house an' I thought you may have had somethin' too heavy for totin' to the curb and needed us to come in ta fetch it fo ya', Mam."

Turning his head quickly away from Mrs. Morley's direction to address the younger man, "Pete go on out to the truck. Eddie needs a hand with Miss Mable's old frig." Jake said finally lifting his eyes from the floor and piercing Pete with a direct commanding glare.

"Please excuse us Mizzus Morley. If there ain't nothin' here mo' for us to tote for ya' we goin' to get on our way." Jake offered with eyes once again immediately cast downward and glued just over the tips of his Brogans. He quickly continued, "Got a heap of work still ahead of us befo' sundown."

"Oh my heavens, mustn't keep hardworking colored menfolk from their work," solicitously smiled Mrs. Morley displaying perfectly white teeth encased in full ruby red lips that hinted of possible miscegenation.

"The boy was just returning my precious locket. I must have dropped it in my haste this morning. After all, haste makes waste." She playfully sung.

"Yes, Mam, it sure do," said Jake attempting to take his leave as quickly as possible.

"Good day, Mam." Jake offered turning on his heels and moving through the heavy wooden doors as swiftly as he came through them only moments ago.

Once on the other side of the massive ornate blocks of wood, Jake exhaled and wiped his forehead relieving it of the perspiration that had gathered. It was a hard sweat brought on by the co-mingling of late morning Southern heat and arrested fear. Eyeing Pete and Eddie a few feet away standing next to the waiting truck; he made a bee-line for the younger man.

"Pete!"

"Boy, hav ya' loss yo' mind!! What in Sam's Hell has gotten into you boy?" Shouted Jake nose to nose in Pete's face. You could've had us all lynched befo' midnight messin' round with that crazy Mizzus Morley. Everybody knows sheeza' Jezebel from the Wes' sida hell! An she gonna burn in hell's fire for all da' trouble she cause roun' heya' thru da' years with colored men folk! Imma have ya switched to another run, boy. Ya on ya way ta Herit' Cah'lage. You gonna be an educated colored boy, not gonna let no loose whitelady de trak ya'… or yo stupidity! Don't know which one of em worse! Go on now, get back up on dis' here truck before I beat your hide my own self!" promised Jake.

"The Lord may not come when or even how you want him; but He's always right on time!" --Grandma Mae

The chirping birds and sun-drenched bedroom made it nearly impossible for Deirdre to ignore the annoying buzz of her alarm clock.

"Ugh," she moaned and flipped over in the overstuffed pillow mattress taking refuge under the soft, peach-toned comforter. It was an early sunny spring Sunday morning and her guilt about her irregular church attendance was starting to get the best of her. She could hear her Grandma Mae, "You know that I raised all of my children to serve the One and Only Living God!" Grandma Mae would harangue without notice or care that her great-grandchildren were even less interested in church attendance than her grandchildren.

Careful not to offend or be accused of disrespecting their elders, the children both young and old would promise the octogenarian that they would be counted among the faithful as soon as life, work, school, basketball, football, volleyball allowed. And of course, it almost never allowed unless the effort to go was intentional. One could always find a legitimate reason for not relinquishing 2 hours of their busy lives every 7 days to worshipping a God that they could not see, taste or touch. Despite Grandma Mae's claims that the Lord could indeed be touched , tasted and seen! "Oh, taste and see that the Lord is good, Chile!" she would proclaim as proof of her belief that God is indeed, real. Nevertheless, Deirdre struggled this spring morning to seek the presence of an invisible God among a throng of seekers meticulously attired with hats and ties in place; hearts and minds ready to receive something that could only be had in an appointed place at an appointed time.

Finally, showered, dressed and perfumed, Deirdre saved the second most challenging Sunday morning ritual for last: Getting her teenage son up and out for church. She wondered sometimes if Moses may have had an easier job of parting the Red Sea.

Tying an apron over her silk blouse and A-line skirt she moved stealthily toward Tommy's bedroom.

"Tommy, it's 8:30am, time to get up for Church! Rise and Shine!" Dee chirps in attempt to at least start the battle on a light note. Deirdre's call is met with a continuation of deep snoozing.

"Tommy! Please get up and come eat your breakfast. It's time for Church," repeats Deirdre now yelling from the kitchen as she turns sizzling turkey bacon over in a caste iron frying pan passed down to her from Grandma Mae.

45 minutes later, despite her relatively good intentions, Deirdre is still running late for church, per usual. Tommy oblivious to his mother's frustration, is literally bouncing in the passenger seat to the latest rap song on his mp3.

"You really need to give that a rest Tommy, you're on your way to Church, boy."

"Brother Charles, Good to see ya! How are you doing today, man?" greets a youthful well-dressed pastor in his late 40's in front of the church with his equally attractive wife.

"I'm good Pastor, real good! Thanks!" says Charles clasping the extended hand of the pastor with his own.

"Got something that I want you to do for the upcoming men's ministry meeting. See me after service, if you can," says the pastor releasing his friendly grip and quickly turning his attention to the congregants flowing up the walkway into the House of Worship. Smiling and exchanging pleasantries, the Reverend and his wife continue their warm greetings and meeting of parishioners until the incoming crowd thins out several minutes later.

Pastor Charles "Chuck" Harris, Jr., III and Minister Patricia Harris came to Mt. Moriah right out of seminary at 28. The youngest minister ever called to the Pastorate in the history of the 130 year old Church. "Pastor Chuck" and his co-laborer, "Minister Pat" immediately won the hearts of the people and continued to endear the flock to both the Gospel and themselves because of their genuine love for seemingly all people.

The Harris' initially came in as interim pastors in the wake of the death of the beloved former senior pastor, Rev. Elijah Mordecai

Smith who at 82 years of age had lead the congregation for over 50 years.

It was Rev. Elijah Mordecai Smith who taught Charles how to pray. He was also the one who personally led him to Christ as a child one summer in Vacation Bible School. The young man's grief over the loss of his life-long pastor was palatable.

1989 was a tough year for the 19 year old. He was tested beyond anything that he could have ever imagined. The death of Pastor Smith just before arriving home to deal with his mom's battle with cancer would have been a lot for even a full grown man of faith. For young Charles, it was nearly devastating. It represented the lost of a Father-figure which re-opened childhood wounds of not ever having had his biological dad in his life. Ernestine Banks, Charles's mom, was his rock. To feel the loss of a father, again, and the eventual death of his mother all in the same year would have been too much had it not been for Rev. Smith's younger successor who helped him emotionally and spiritually navigate one of the greatest storms of his young life. Rev. Smith gave him the tool of prayer. Pastor Chuck taught him how to use his tool as a weapon of faith against the enemy of his heart and mind. Walking out his faith in the fiery furnace of grief, loss, depression and heartbreak. He taught him how to overcome. So there wasn't too much that Pastor Chuck or the Church could ask of him — after all, he had saved his life.

Settling into his favorite spot, Charles took his seat near the back of the church.

"Good morning, Sweetie," an elderly woman smiles at Charles showing perfect dentured teeth.

"Good morning, Mother Clarke. How are you?" Charles quickly responds moving down the pew to get close enough to plant a kiss on the older woman's powdered cheek.

"Fine, Baby, How are you?"
You really grew up to be a fine young man. I'm so proud of you!"

"Thank you, Mother Clarke" Charles humbly responds. Without solicitation the elder offers, "You know you were a bad little somethin' when you was younger? Your Mama use to take you downstairs in that bathroom and wear your little behind out," the woman chuckles as she reminisces.

"Yeah, I remember those days Mother Clarke," Charles offers sharing the older woman's amusement.

"Now look at ya', All grown up. What are you about 35?"

"38, Mother Clarke. Just turned 38 on my last birthday about a month ago."

"Lord have mercy! Time sure does fly! ," she exclaims. "So have you found yourself a nice girl to marry yet, son? Mrs. Clarke asks conspiratorially leaning into Charles in a hushed voice that gets drowned out by the church organist as the processional starts. Thankful for the interruption, Charles lightly squeezes the older woman's hand and bids her a polite farewell as the church music overtakes the last syllables of their conversation.

There was something familiar about the woman and her teenage son, but Charles couldn't quite make the connection. He hadn't noticed either of them come into the sanctuary but could not stop looking at them once becoming aware of them. He saw so many people on the daily basis between work, running in and out of libraries for school over the years, church and community volunteering — who knew? He tried his best to ignore them, but the kid kept distracting his mother, just like he use to do in church as a 13 or 14 year old. He dropped his head slightly and chuckled because the woman's reaction to her teenage son's antics were exactly the same as his mother's over two and a half decades ago.

When Pastor Chuck invited the congregation to the altar for prayer, the woman met with some obvious resistance made her way to the altar with her son. Moved to go to the altar himself this Sunday, Charles filed out of the pew a couple of rows behind the twosome and also headed for the Throne of Grace.

Not quite sure why he came to the altar, Charles just bowed his head, closed his eyes and listened to the Pastor's prayer and the chorus of prayers that floated around him.

"Amen." He echoed as Pastor Chuck ended the prayer and all who gathered around the altar rose and returned to their seats echoing their own "Amens!" and "Hallelujahs!"

The service moved to an uncharacteristically quick close. Worshippers streamed out of the ecclesiastical edifice as casually as they entered. Some looked a little more relaxed than they did a couple of hours earlier. Deirdre for one, was counted among the "look betters." Church service had a way of making everything in her world alright and giving her just what she needed to fight her way through the week ahead until the next Sunday.

"Hey Mom, there's that guy who bought me pizza at the mall!" Tommy points out in Charles' direction as they move along with the crowd toward the stained glass embellished wooden doors of the outer sanctuary.

"Stop pointing, Tommy. It's rude," counters Deirdre.

"But, Mom look! It's really him!" the teen implores. Deirdre glances in the direction of Tommy's attention and admits that the gentleman did indeed look vaguely familiar. "Tommy, he certainly looks familiar, but I don't think that's the man from the mall," observes Deirdre as her eyes meet Charles' from a short distance.

"The Food Court at the mall," whispers Charles to himself.

"That's where I know them from!" The hint of recognition suddenly registers propelling Charles to move toward the woman and her son. Before he fully realized what he had done, he found himself standing directly in front of Deirdre with his hand offered.

"Hi, I'm Charles Monroe. I think I met you and your son not too long ago at the Food Court in the mall."

"French fries with pizza! Right, my man?" Charles reminds Tommy, sharing a quick laugh with the teen.

"Yeah!" Tommy smiles back at Charles amused.

"See, I told you that he was the guy, Ma!" the teen says turning to his mother like he just won a contest.

"And you remember that he tried to order fries with pizza? I can hardly remember what day of the week it is. Wow!" Deirdre chuckles as people attempt to move around the threesome who were now blocking the flow of human traffic coming out of the building.

"Looks like we're in the way here. Where are you guys parked? Can I walk you to your car?" offers Charles.

"Sure," smiles Deirdre comfortably as Tommy shyly smirks at his mom's instantly softened persona and mannerisms.

"Are you a member of Mt. Moriah?" Charles inquires.

"No, but I have been a regular visitor for longer than I care to admit," confesses Deirdre with a hint of embarrassment.

"How about you?" she asks.

"Born and raised." Charles answers with pride. He continues, "I literally grew up here. Lots of memories."

"I bet," says Deirdre. "It's a wonderful fellowship of believers. I don't know what stops me from officially joining. I guess I don't want to commit until I am sure that it is the right place for me and my son."

"Well how long have you been an 'incognito visitor?" teases Charles.

"Oh, about 3 years," admits Deirdre.

"Three years?" echoes Charles.

"Guess I have some commitment issues, eh?" laughs Deirdre.

"Well, I won't be too quick to judge you; but something is going on there." Charles offers lightly as they approach Deirdre's car.

"Hey, it was nice meeting you." Deirdre says extending a manicured hand in Charles' direction who receives it without releasing it immediately.

"Perhaps the three of us could go grab something to eat one Sunday after service?" Suggests Charles.

"Sure, that would be nice." Says Deirdre accepting the future invitation.

"How about now?" chimes in Tommy. "I'm starvin'!"

"Boy, you're always hungry! No, we're not going today."

"Oh! Why not, Mom?" Pleads Tommy.

"Why not, Mom? Charles playfully repeats with a smile that disarms the clearly out voted mom.

"I mean, if now isn't a good time, perhaps another Sunday?" He quickly counter-offers in attempt to avoid being perceived as being too forward in his spontaneous, but genuine request.

"Now, Mom, Pleeeasse!" begs Tommy. "I'm soooooooo hungry,' the teen exaggerates.

"Oh, stop it boy!" Deirdre chides her son.

"O.K. Why not?" Deirdre gives in happily finally freeing her hand from Charles' gentle hold to open her car door.

"Where are you parked? We'll follow you."

"Mom, I really like this guy," announces Tommy as he dives into the passenger seat of the car with the exuberance of youth that can only come with a 13 year old boy courting puberty.

"You should make him your boyfriend and then the two of you should get married!" Tommy states in a matter-of-fact manner and visibly happy with his summary of future events. The teen buckles up and rolls down the window on his side of the car and continues,

"Pastor Chuck could do the wedding." He sits up rod straight in the passenger seat.

"And now you may kiss the prize!" the teen clowns attempting to imitate the baritone and cadence of the Pastor.

"That's kiss the bride, silly!"

"Same difference," quips Tommy as he deftly produces earphones and his mp3 out of thin air and goes back to his pre-empted bouncing to the "other" preachers of the hour.

"And how are you marrying me off to a complete stranger?"

"Well, you're going to a restaurant with a complete stranger," counters Tommy.

"Besides we know him from the mall and he bought me pizza; so he's not really a stranger." Tommy says turning up the volume of his electronic device this time hoping to successfully drown his mom's voice out for as long as possible. Feeling lighter in spirit than she has felt in a long time, Deirdre clicks on her favorite CD and hums along as she and her son follow the immaculate sedan in front of them being driven by a man that she just met at church.

"So, what's everyone having today?" asks the waiter as she simultaneously places three cool glasses of water on the table.

"Food! And plenty of it!" jokes Charles. "You have two hungry men here and a young lady who looks like she has a decent appetite," teases Charles.

"Excuse me, Sir?
But what exactly is that suppose to mean?" Deirdre playfully challenges.

"You don't strike me as the dainty type, Maam. Which is good," counters Charles with a smile.

"I'm not sure how to take that." Deirdre responds as she notices Tommy grinning from ear to ear with his head following their dialog like he's watching a tennis match. Deirdre interrupts her repartee with Charles to check Tommy.

"And what are you grinning about?" she challenges her son.

"Oh, nothing!" he says in a sing-song way.

"This is fun!" Tommy enthuses looking at his mother and then to Charles and back to his mother again. Once the orders are taken and the jovial banter subsides, Deirdre in a more serious tone asks,

"So tell me about yourself, Mr. Monroe." Allowing his eyes to rest on the sincere interest that he sees in Deirdre's expression, Charles clears his throat and begins.

" Well, this is my hometown, been here all of my life. I attended Heritage College at 16 and dropped out at 19 in the spring of my Junior year to take care of my mother who was dying of cancer at the time."

"Oh, I'm so sorry." Deirdre offers with genuine compassion.

"Thanks. That was nearly 20 years ago."

"So what do you do?" Asks Deirdre of the clean-cut gentleman in front of her.

"I'm a sanitation worker. I've been with the Department 20 years." Answers Charles not able to ignore the look of surprise that registers on Deirdre's face. Before he can say another word, Deirdre apologizes.

"I'm sorry. My face must have registered shock."

"So, you're a garbage man, Charles?" Tommy innocently asks.

"That's Mr. Monroe to you, mister," corrects Deirdre.

"Wow! I thought you were a lawyer or a professor or businessman like my dad," Tommy continues.

"Tommy, please."

"I'm sorry." Deirdre offers.

"Why are you apologizing? My man, just gave me a compliment," says Charles totally unfettered by the last few awkward moments of conversation.

"It happens all the time when people initially meet me. I'm kind of bookish and most folks do not expect any level of intellectualism to be connected to one who picks up other peoples garbage for a living. And how about you? Where did you go to school? What do you do for a living?" Charles asks without waning interest.

"I attended a small liberal arts college in New England on full academic scholarship and have a degree in Business Administration."

"Wow! So you're a smart sistah!"

"I'm alright." Deirdre chuckles lightly.

"You're no slouch yourself, Heritage Man! What did you study?" Deirdre asks shifting the attention back on Charles and away from herself.

"I was working on a double major in History and English Literature when I left and happy to say that after 20 long years am just 6 credits away from my degree."

"Awesome! Congratulations!"

"Yeah, congratulations Charles! Uh, I mean Mr. Monroe," chimes in Tommy.

"Thanks, my Man!" Charles says giving Tommy a fist pound of agreement.

"So, let me guess. That makes you around 38?" Inquires Deirdre.

"Yes indeed, Maam. Just celebrated my 38th birthday a month ago. God is good!" Charles proclaims with unreserved enthusiasm.

Clearing her throat as she picks up her glass of water Deirdre quietly agrees, "Yes, He is."

Somewhat preoccupied with the most recent information gathered in their conversation, Deirdre turns her attention to the plate of food that has just been set in front of her. Bowing her head after giving Tommy 'the look' for grabbing one of his fries and quickly popping it into his mouth, she waits for Charles to grace the table.

A few moments of silence pass as the three hungrily dig into omelettes, fried potatoes, sausage, bacon, toast dripping with butter, a cheeseburger and fries, with an assortment of beverages dispersed around the table.

"I'm stuffed," declares Charles reclining back into the booth, grabbing a napkin off the previously food laden table. He moves the napkin deftly across the lower portion of his clean shaven face and angular chin and asks, "Well partner in crime, how was that cheeseburger and fries?" looking to Tommy whose body is almost perpendicular to the chair he was sitting upright in prior to the meal.

"Boy, Sit up! You're not at home." Deirdre says tapping the teen on the shoulder for emphasis. Adjusting immediately, Tommy dramatically proclaims, "That was the best cheeseburger in the history of all cheeseburgers!" The teen says saluting Charles.

"You're quite a character, aren't you?" You're not a shy kid; you've really got your own thing going on, my man. I like that." Charles assesses.

"He certainly does," adds Deirdre rolling her eyes heaven-ward as she gathers her bag and Tommy's long ago abandoned necktie from the floor beneath his seat. The boy grins ear to ear taking in the older man's compliment and a new calmness that he's never before seen in this mother.

"So, Madame Deirdre," says Charles turning his full attention in her direction lingering briefly with a gentle smile on the composition of her features before speaking again.

"Are you satisfied?"

"Excuse me?" Questions Deirdre, not quite sure how to respond.

"Did you enjoy your meal?" Charles re-phrases wondering what was going through her mind.

"Oh, yes." Deirdre recovers.

"Thank you."

"And you?" she returns the politeness.

"Great!" Says Charles retrieving his wallet from the inside of this suit jacket that was discarded to the back of a nearby chair when the three arrived at the restaurant nearly an hour and a half ago.

"Well, that certainly was a meal fit for a king!" Deirdre says turning to Charles once outside and headed for their parked vehicles.

"And a queen," Charles gently adds causing Deirdre to blush slightly. "And a prince!" Tommy chimes in not allowing himself to be left out. Deirdre and Charles look at the teen then at each other and laugh. As they reach Deirdre's car she extends her hand in gratitude to the gentleman standing in front of her.

"Charles, we really had a wonderful time. Thanks so much."

"The pleasure was indeed mine, Lovely Lady." Charles responds taking Deirdre in fully for the hundredth time in the last hour as he lifts her hand and plants a gentle kiss on it. To Tommy's absolute delight, Charles quickly adds, "And to the prince." Releasing Deirdre's hand but not her attention as he turns to shake her son's hand and bid farewell.

"Never be afraid to ask God for what you want, baby. But don't ever forget that He already knows what you need."

--Grandma Mae

Several weeks later...

Deirdre knew that Charles had to be in his mid to late 30's and hit the nail on the head when she guessed his age to be about 38 the first time they went out together when she and Tommy joined him after Church for brunch. The ten year difference made no difference in Charles' growing attraction to Deirdre. Nevertheless, he was a little surprised to learn that she was not 40 or even 41; but 48. Yet, Deirdre struggled with the idea of dating a man 10 years her junior.

"My mother was 7 years older than my father and they had a beautiful relationship," shares Deirdre's best friend Janice in attempt to ease her friend's anxiety.

"Jan, your parents are from another planet! They're like something straight out of the '50's!" Deirdre refutes exasperated.

"What am I saying?" she questions herself without wanting or waiting for an answer.

"They are straight out of the 1950's!"

"Dee, true love and commitment is love and commitment no matter what the age or time. Real love is timeless and without our human boundaries and limitations. That's why it is so wonderful!" Janice finishes satisfied.

"Leave it to you to wax poetic in the middle of my romantic crisis!"

"You see that's your problem, Dee. You over romanticize everything."

"Me? Over romanticizing? Oh, Please!"

"Yes, you have these unrealistic ideas about love and relationships. Yet, at the same time you operate under all of these self-imposed restraints." Jan continues, "Who says that love must only be shared between two people who are the same age? A 7 to 10 year difference doesn't make a difference if everyone is grown! Now, if you were trying to get together with this man 20 years ago when you were 28 and he was 18; THAT would have been a problem!" Laughs Jan.

"You're not funny," says Deirdre.

"Yes, I am." Counters Jan, laughing some more.

"Well, Miss Comedian, I have to get off the phone now. Charles invited me over to his place to watch a movie or two."

"Oh, big spender!" Teases Jan. "Home movies already, eh?"

"Oh stop it," says Deirdre. "You know I prefer watching movies at home to the theatre anyway." Deirdre says with a hint of annoyance. Continuing, "And so far he has shown himself to be pretty generous. We've only been dating a little over a month and he has picked up

every tab, so far," she states matter-of-factly. "Speaking of the angel, he just sent me a text that he's on his way. Gotta' go!"

"Call me tomorrow." Adds Deirdre.

"Will do, Stella!" teases Janice laughing again as they both release their respective phone lines.

There was no doubt in Deirdre's heart or mind that she was growing more attracted to Charles by the minute. Despite her reservations about their age difference, she certainly did not feel any gap in intellect, conversation or demeanor. When with Charles all she saw and felt was a strong and compassionate man who knew his own heart and mind and respected the hearts and minds of others. Unique. And on top of all of that, he had a way of looking at her that made her cognizant of her femininity—her Womaness. His pensive and appreciative assessments of her touched and softened something deep inside of Deirdre that she could neither explain nor ignore. It thrilled, yet unnerved her. She even questioned the wisdom of getting together with him at his house for the first time alone without Tommy in tow. Having her son around kind of helped put the brakes on the crazy impulses that she was feeling when in the presence of a man that truly made her feel things that she thought she'd never feel again.

"Hey, beautiful, I'm here," says Charles calling from his car. "Do you want me to come in or should I wait?" he asks.

"I'll be right out," says Deirdre hurriedly clicking the phone back to her conversation with her son. She reminds him to behave at his father's house, be respectful toward his step-mother, read his Bible and say his prayers.

"Hey." Says Deirdre as she slips into the passenger seat of Charles' sedan. Charles taking her in fully before speaking says,

"Hey, yourself."

"Umph, you could really get a righteous brother in a lot of trouble," Charles half mumbles to himself as he puts the car in drive and heads across town. Intentionally changing his focus, Charles offers,

"I ordered take-out from Louie's Pasta House since you really liked it when we were there for dinner last week."

"Oh, that sounds good! I love Louie's!" says Deirdre unconsciously fanning herself and thankful for the break in the tension she's feeling.

"What movie are we watching?" inquires Deirdre taking in Charles' profile, noting the smooth angles that denote his rugged good-looks. Looking Deirdre full in the face once again, he says,

"Anything you desire, my Lovely Lady, we can download it from my service." Unnerved by the sudden impulse that she feels just to touch Charles, Deirdre once again regains her composure.

"I'm in the mood for a Tyler Perry movie!" I feel like laughing!" she announces.

"As you like," smiles Charles. "Then we'll watch something with some good chase scenes, fights and explosions," says Charles.

"Fair enough," concedes Deirdre resisting the urge to fan herself once again.

"Have I ever told you that I find you absolutely beautiful?" asks Charles.

"Yes, you have Charles. But more than what you say to me is how you treat me. So yes, you have hundreds of times."

"Good." Says Charles as he pulls into his driveway; shuts off his car and gives Deirdre the look that sends her mind wheeling and her impulses whirling; and the evening was just beginning! She wasn't sure if she was going to make it until the end of the evening without doing something crazy. As if on cue, Charles interrupts his own wandering thoughts and smiles gently.

"We should probably go inside."

"Of course," says Deirdre feeling a short-lived sense of relief. Charles gets out of the car first and swiftly moves to the passenger side to open Deirdre's door. Deirdre takes the few seconds alone in the car to exhale. "This is going to be interesting," she whispers audibly to herself. Charles in an instant appears opening her door with an extended hand helping her out of the vehicle.

"Thank you," says Deirdre.

"My pleasure," responds Charles as they walk hand in hand up the pathway that leads to the front door of his house. Neither noticing that they had not released the other's hand until Charles needs to retrieve his keys to open the door. Ushering Deirdre into the foyer of his well-kept abode; he points her in the direction of the

Family Room as he veers off to the left to get their meal from the kitchen.

"I am really impressed with how well you keep your home; for a guy." Deirdre teasingly calls out to Charles from the cozy room that looks like a mini-home theatre with a large screen TV that nearly covers one of the plum-colored walls.

"Then I've succeeded," replies Charles from the kitchen as he grabs eating utensils and places them on a tray filled with an assortment of aromatic pasta dishes and heads in Deirdre's direction.

"Oh my goodness! You have enough food to feed an army!" exclaims Deirdre as she makes room for Charles and the Italian feast on the couch.

"Dining fit for a king and his queen," Charles smiles bringing back a recent memory of their first date. Deirdre smiles as well over a slight blush and grabs the two empty ceramic plates and begins serving both herself and Charles from the large platter.

"Indeed it is," says Deirdre handing Charles the first filled plate with a napkin and utensils.

"Thanks," says Charles receiving the food and the kindness of his guest. Settling back on the couch shoulder to shoulder they both bow their heads as Charles blesses the meal.

"Amen. Let's eat!" Jokes Deirdre.

"Amen to that!" Charles agrees.

"Ummm, this tastes as good as it looks!" proclaims Deirdre as she digs into the savory hot food.

"Agreed." Charles chuckles as he takes a quick bite from his plate and gets up to program the movie. Half-way through the meal they both confess that they are stuffed; surrender their plates to the large mahogany coffee table in front of them and attempt to watch the movie. Content and cozy, Deirdre slightly adjusts herself and settles comfortably into Charles' arms on the oversized couch. Pleased with her relaxed state, he draws her in for greater comfort. With his arm securely around her, Deirdre uses the breadth of his broad chest as a place to rest her head. Smiling again, Charles lightly strokes Deirdre's hair with his free hand, gently running his fingers through the soft dark strands. The movie although entertaining feels like a backdrop to their on-going conversation. Laughing about a scene in the film, Charles confesses,

"Something like that happened to me."

"No way!" Laughs Deirdre. "I don't believe it!" she says lightly pushing her index finger into his chest for emphasis.

"Believe it, baby," states Charles taking her hand into his and gently kissing it as he pulls her yet closer and begins to tell his story.

"It was about 10 years after my mom passed. I had just purchased this house. 28 years old, single, brand new house and a spanking brand new car. Not bad for a brother that had to drop out of college. I was THE MAN! Was doing my thing with the ladies before, but my stock went through the roof with the new house and car. About six months before I closed on the house, I was in Atlanta for my old college roomie, Rick's baby's Christening. He and his wife, Donna asked me to be the baby's Godfather so I took off a week and just made a vacation out of it." Charles continues with Deirdre's full attention, "Right after dinner, me and couple of the guys left the family man at home with his wife and kid and went roamin'. Hit all the main spots. We were clubbin' like it was 1999, because it was!" He chuckles to himself reminiscing. "Meant this fine sistah named Porsche at MoodyBlues. She was a public relations specialist for some big non-profit organization in Manhattan. This sistah had a body that made a grown man dizzy, with a cute little face to match! Just so happens she was from NY down in Atlanta visiting some friends. We chatted, exchanged numbers, hooked up a couple of times that week and continued seeing each other when we got back home.

I was a young single man doing my thing not really too concerned with getting into anything crazy with her or any woman at that time. We were seeing each other just about every other weekend until I bought my house. All of the sudden she gets real clingy and starts talking all this marriage talk that I seriously wasn't trying to hear. Every other weekend turned into every weekend that morphed into her commuting to work in Manhattan from my house almost every week." Charles pauses to interject,

"I had so much drama back in those days it wasn't even funny." He continues, "Anyway, about a month after I bought the house my buddy Ty falls out with the woman that he had been living with for 5 years. She put him out one night in the middle of the night!" Charles laughs. "So, whose door do you think he comes knocking on at 3 in the morning?" Charles asks and then continues. "He moves in with me for almost a year splitting the mortgage. It actually ended up being a sweet deal at the time; it allowed me to get ahead of some of the debt that I had incurred in furnishing the house and putting the deck out back. So, here we are two single brothers with a big enough house to do anything we thought we were big and bad enough to do. It was crazy! With the exception of Porsche's increasingly annoying chatter about us getting married, I felt like I had died and gone to heaven. Then Porsche announces one Friday night while we're out grabbing a bite to eat, that she missed her period. I'm like, "And???" After she calls me everything that a sistah with African and Latino blood running equally through her veins can think of... You know, I think that girl cursed me out in two or three different languages." Charles reflects. "Have you ever been cursed out bilingually?" Charles asks Deirdre who is totally engrossed in his tale. She silently nods her head, "No," as he continues, "So, she cusses me out and leaves my house with her overnight bag. As soon as the door slammed I proceeded to go through the house collecting all of her little girly items randomly strewn throughout the house like she lived here or something. Nail polish bottles next to the couch in the living room, curling iron in the bathroom, a sweatsuit on the back of the chair in my bedroom, hair clips and fasteners everywhere that you could imagine! Even feminine hygiene products under the bathroom sink! I packed it all up, took it out of my house and put it in the trunk of my car.

"Oh, no you didn't!" exclaims Deirdre laughing.

"Believe me, I knew that I would see her at least one more time." Says Charles matter-of-factly. "That Sunday when the preacher invited anyone that wanted to come for prayer to the altar, I think I almost knocked over one of the old church ladies trying to get up there. I fell to my knees and prayed like I was 10 years old again begging God to not let my mother take me off the baseball team for breaking Miss Mary's car window playing stick ball with rocks out on the street with Johnny Jones. I'll never forget that boyhood prayer or the one that I prayed as a young man at that same altar that Sunday,

"Lord, if you just give me another chance I promise I won't sleep with another woman who isn't my wife. You know that I want to get married and have a family one day, Lord. But this is not the way I wanted to do it. Please Lord, I don't want to do to a child what my dad did to me... Lord you know my heart, you know that I don't love Porsche like a man should love a woman he wants to marry. I was wrong. Lord, I'm sorry. You've given me everything and I don't want to blow it. Please fix this situation for me and

help me to live right. In Jesus' Name I pray. Amen."

Well, by the time that I got back to my seat, I honestly felt like my prayer had been heard. Didn't know exactly what the Lord had done on my behalf, but I had a feeling that everything was going to be alright! About a week later, Porsche calls for the first time since our blow-up. I didn't even try to call her, I knew she'd call.

"We need to talk." She said.

"Yes, I know." I said.

"Umm, how you feeling?" I asked her.

"How am I feeling, Charles? You're asking me how I'm feeling? How do you think I'm feeling?" she asked without waiting for a response. "Here I am thinking that you love me, and that we might one day get married and have children together, be a family...," her voice slightly cracked as she paused to compose herself. The upset woman continued, " that I might even have been carrying your son or daughter right now and you act like you could give a flying pair of trousers!" She ranted.

"I was silent." Charles confesses. Hesitant, I uttered, "Well, umm have you seen a doctor, are you pregnant?"

"For your information Mr. Monroe, I am not pregnant. The doctor thinks that it was work related stress and possibly the recent commuting from New Jersey into Manhattan that may have stressed me to the point of delaying my menstrual cycle. I hope you're happy!"

Relieved that both the rant and the baby scare were over I politely found a way to end the conversation much to Porsche's chagrin. Her personal items stayed in my trunk for almost 9 months. I never heard from her again so I dumped them in one of the trucks that was heading out one morning as I was coming into the garage to report for work.

Shortly after that, Ty found an apartment in-town and moved out. He said that my new self-imposed "no-overnight-honey's rule" was giving him the weebee-jeebies and that it was getting harder and harder for him to do his thing when he knew that I wasn't doing mine. So for the betterment of getting his groove on and our friendship he moved out and got his own place. That was 10 years ago almost to this very day, and I haven't slept with, fondled or sexually had a woman in my bed, on my couch, backseat of my car… God knows this is a hard promise to keep," Charles finishes looking directly at Deirdre as he softly runs his hand across the smoothness of her face. Before she can stop herself she reaches out and gently touches the fullness of his lips with the tip of her finger. Too afraid to allow herself to do anything more. Charles equally challenged, but outwardly a lot more composed, continues,

"That's why I decided around the same time to also renew my promise to finish my degree that I made to my mother. Working full-time and being in school helped keep my mind occupied… but you know temptation will follow a brotha' wherever he goes. Yes,

I've been tempted a whole lot to break my promise to God and my mother… but I can truly say that the Lord has given me the strength to keep both over the past ten years."

"Good story!" smiles Deirdre as she slightly shifts creating a little space between her and Charles.

"Where ya' going?" he asks.

"Oh, I need to use the bathroom," she quickly offers standing over him smoothing her denim dress after he helps her up from the couch. Charles doesn't move another muscle as he intently watches Deirdre make her exit from the room and disappear into the hallway. It's the sound of the closing bathroom door that jolts him out of his reverie back into the moment. He unconsciously releases a slight groan and pleads, "Lord, have mercy on a brotha'!" Rising abruptly in attempt to change the direction of his thoughts, Charles changes the movie. "Make my day, Mr. Eastwood; make my day," he chuckles lightly to himself.

Taking refuge in the small room that matches the larger room that she just left; Deirdre carefully closes the door. Sighing with her back against the hardwood, she looks upward,

"Ok God, you obviously have a sense of humor." She swallows hard. "10 year age difference and celibate?" She questions.

"And Lord, if I have to deal with all of this you at least didn't have to make him so dang fine! Lord have mercy! What exactly am I suppose to do?" Deirdre pleads with an unseen but at this very moment more felt than ever, God.

"Ok, your way, Lord. Not mine." Deirdre concedes deciding to quickly splash some cool water on her face and rinse her mouth before returning to Charles in the next room.

"I'm back," she announces re-entering the cozy room to find Charles patiently awaiting her return. With the movie remote dangling from one hand and his arm resting peacefully on the back of the couch, he beckons,

"Indeed you are," he says smiling warmly and patting the empty spot on the couch next to him. "Come, let's watch some good chase scenes and fights," he teases.

"Sounds good to me." Deirdre happily agrees.

"Thought I heard you in there talking? Who were you talking to?" Charles playfully inquires.

"I was praying." Deirdre admits.

"Hmmm," responds Charles thoughtfully.

"Had to whisper one up in here myself." They knowingly look at each other and laugh as Deirdre resumes her comfy position in Charles arms and they attempt once again to watch a movie. There is less talking this time around. Deirdre tries to be a good sport and watch the movie but falls asleep half way through. Charles completely relaxed and engrossed in the film doesn't even notice that she has fallen asleep in his arms until he announces that he is headed for the kitchen to get something to drink.

"Do you want anything from the kitchen?" Charles asks looking down on Deirdre's sleepy head not realizing that she is in a deep snooze. When she doesn't respond, Charles eases back gently turning her face toward him and realizes that Deirdre is asleep. He carefully re-adjusts so that he can slip away without disturbing her peaceful repose, propping her legs with care up on the couch in the spot that he just left. Now face to face from a kneeling position on the floor in front of the couch, Charles is unable to resist the pure serenity he sees in Deirdre's tranquil slumber. Tenderly touching her face once again he rises from the kneeling position that he assumed to make the sleeping woman on his couch more comfortable, and heads for the kitchen. Whistling softly down the hallway, he makes his way to the frig and gets a cold drink. On the way back he grabs a blanket from the hallway closet. Upon re-entering the room, Charles clicks off the movie and turns on some soft jazz and gives his full attention to covering Deirdre with the blanket under his arm. Once done, he eases back into place on the couch scooping the sleeping woman into his arms and soon dozes off himself; content and satisfied.

Close to an hour later Deirdre stirs and awakens momentarily disoriented. Feeling the weight of Charles arms around her she smiles realizing exactly where she is and reaches for her bag on the floor next to the couch. Digging through the leather sack, she finds her phone and checks the time. "Oh my, it's after midnight already!" Deirdre says to herself surprised and wondering just how long she has been sleeping. Taking in the peaceful repose of the sleeping man who has her securely wrapped in his arms, she gently frees herself from his embrace and begins to gather her things in preparation to leave. After locating her discarded shoes underneath the couch and her jacket on a nearby chair, Deirdre tiptoes into the bathroom to tidy up before waking Charles.

"Dee?" She hears Charles call out to her from the other room.

"I'm in the bathroom, Charles," noting the unexpected use of her nickname.

"I was trying not to disturb you," she says re-entering the room.

"You looked so peaceful." She adds.

"Hmmmmmh," Charles audibly releases as he yawns and stretches; still a little groggy from the late night nap.

"You look ready to leave." He assesses watching Deirdre fasten her jacket.

"Yeah, it's pretty late."

"Or early, depending on how you choose to see it," says Charles with a hint of mischief. "Why not stay until the morning and we'll have breakfast together?" Charles suggests. Deirdre with a quizzical look declines.

"Um, based on everything that you shared with me tonight, I don't think an overnight or until morning stay is an option, Sir."

"Oh woman, please. I see you have a one-track mind," Charles teases.

"Come," he says beckoning her back to the couch. "Sit. We don't have to leave right this minute." Taking her hand in his larger hands he looks at her for a moment before speaking.

"Look , Dee." Realizing that he called her "Dee" and not Deirdre, he adds, "Can I call you Dee?" Deirdre nods, "Yes, my family and close friends all call me Dee."

"Well, I certainly would like to be counted among those that you consider close relations." Charles says with a gentleness that matches the sincerity in his eyes.

"Of course." Offers Deirdre.

"Good." Responds Charles softly caressing her hand in his before releasing it to grab his keys.

"Ok, my Lovely Lady, let's get you home before we both turn into pumpkins," Charles jokes rising up from the sofa and then helping Deirdre to do the same. Turning off the lights as they leave, he leads Deirdre out of the room. Just as they reach the front door to exit the house, Charles remembers that he forgot something and quickly turns back and goes toward the Family Room.

"Tommy left his basketball game the last time you were here," informs Charles returning to the foyer with a couple of video games in hand.

"Tell him I want a re-match," he laughs handing Deirdre the games.

"There are two; he only brought one over," recounts Deirdre looking at the newer game with curiosity.

"He won that in our match," offers Charles.

"But it's brand new. It hasn't even been opened yet." Observes Deirdre.

"Yep. I know," says Charles not offering any more on the subject matter.

"Thanks," says Deirdre sheepishly. "That's really kind of you."

"No problem, Lovely Lady," Charles shrugs relaxed and now standing comfortably with his hands in his pockets directly in front of Deirdre.

"You have a great kid," he adds.

"Good job you're doing, Mama," Charles smiles bending slightly in Deirdre's direction and placing a light kiss on her forehead. Visibly surprised by the spontaneous gesture, Deirdre searches Charles' peaceful countenance. Aware of her sudden discomfort, Charles releases his hands from his pockets and allows them to rest on Deirdre's shoulders.

"What's the matter, Dee?" Charles asks sincerely searching her questioning face for answers.

"Nothing, Charles," she softly responds careful not to take her eyes off the pools of compassion that flow from his.

"I can make it better, baby," promises Charles taking in the rhythm of her breathing as she struggles to keep her emotions in check.

"I'm sure that you probably can." Quietly agrees Deirdre as Charles gently brings her face to his and kisses her softly.

"If you let me, Deirdre." Charles adds seeking confirmation in her tearing eyes. Moving his fingers slowly across the fullness of her lips; he pulls her to himself a second time and kisses her again; this time more deeply. Deirdre allowing herself to feel her slightly smaller stature melt into his embrace; meets the force of Charles' passion with her own as a single tear gently escapes her control. Both fully spent and a bit overwhelmed by the flood of emotion; stand quietly holding each other in the silence of the wee hour in the stillness of the night. After a long moment, Deirdre reluctantly breaks the embrace in effort to regain a modicum of self-control. However, the moment her eyes meet Charles', she knows that things will never be the same between them and that self-control is going to be an issue in the days and very long nights ahead.

"Let's get out of here," Charles says breaking into her thoughts placing a light kiss on top of her head. Without another word,

Deirdre silently nods her agreement and allows Charles to lead her out of the house. Charles deep in thought most of the short journey across town; occasionally checks in on the uncharacteristically silent woman sitting next to him in the passenger seat.

"You Ok?" he asks.

Nodding her head "Yes," Deirdre gives him a half-smile for assurance and turns back to her private thoughts. Pulling up in front of Deirdre's house, Charles turns the overhead light on so that he can see her face. He then shuts the car off to her surprise.

"It's after 1am in the morning, don't want to disturb your neighbors." Charles offers sensing Deirdre's confusion.

"Oh." She responds. "That's very considerate of you. I was wondering what you were doing," she nervously admits.

"Good night, Charles," says Deirdre letting herself out of the car.

"Good night, Deirdre," warmly responds Charles allowing his eyes to rest on her face.

"Goodnight, my Lovely Lady," whispers Charles mostly to himself as he watches Deirdre leave the car and move up the short pathway to her front door. He lingers a moment longer until he sees a light come on inside the house. Satisfied, he restarts his car and drives off returning to his own home with a head full of thoughts and a heart that's burgeoning with a greater new hope.

"A man must have some space to just be a man with other men or we'll forget who we are."

--Great Uncle Julius Monroe

Charles missed the last 'Boys' Night' at Ty's. It was his Movie Night with Deirdre at his house and his first opportunity to be alone with her since they started seeing each other. Ty and the boys are relentless in their questioning and teasing.

"Hey Man, are you still doing that religious "No Sex" thing?" Asks Ty. Charles semi-glaring over his cards, just nods affirmatively without a word.

"Have you met the Professor's new Ole' Lady?" Ty says turning to Carlos who sits adjacent to him preoccupied with grabbing potato chips with his one free hand while closely studying his cards.

"No pun intended, man!" Ty laughs continuing,

"Dee Dee, Deborah…"

"Deirdre, man. Her name is Deirdre." Charles corrects.

"Hey, my brotha', I ain't mad at ya'! I see what you see, my man." Playfully concedes Ty .

"She's a little bit old for my son here," Ty continues with his teasing. "But the sistah is fine. Holdin' it down for a 40-something."

"40-something?" questions Eddie the designated card dealer for the night who up until now has remained silent.

"Really?" looking to Charles.

"Yeah, man." Nods Charles.

"Nawh man, I haven't been introduced to my man's new lady." Says Carlos finally able to get a word in between Ty's repartee.

"You didn't tell me that you were hooked up, Bro'." Carlos says in Charles' direction.

"Yeah, I did man. You just don't remember." Counters Charles taking his turn and gesturing to Eddie for another card.

"How can he remember anything with all that racket his kids keep up in his house!" says Eddie as he flips the requested card to Charles.

"My children have VIDA ABUNDANTE! Just like their Padre!" Carlos announces with pride.

"Yep. And that's why Maria is always at my house with my wife trying to get a break from all of ya'll!" laughs Eddie.

"You know they ignore your calls and text messages, man?" Eddie digs.

"Oh, no man! My Maria is loyal!" Carlos proclaims in self defense.

"I'm telling you what I know, man. I hear them laughing and talking in the kitchen. When Maria's cell phone goes off she says, "Ay, Caramba! Can't get a break from this man and his children! They're about to make me loco, Priscilla!" Eddie says imitating Carlos' wife. The room cracks up in laughter.

"No es verdad, man. You lie." Carlos says self-assured and taking his turn in the game.

"Remember that fine Public Relations workin' sistah you met down in Atlanta?" Ty starts up again.

"Patty, Penelope, Pookie…?"

"Her name was Porsche, man." Charles corrects for the second time tonight.

"Yeah! Yeah!" Recalls Ty as if though he knew all along.

"Oh yeah, Bro'! I remember that Mamacita! Whew! Muy Caliente!" Carlos chimes in high-fiving Ty.

"Now that was a sistah a brotha' could really settle down with," Ty pauses for dramatic effect and then continues.

"At least every night, again in the morning, with a few quickies in between!" Howls Ty with Carlos' full agreement.

"Man, you've got issues," Charles says shaking his head in mock disgust.

"Naawh! Man, I am perfectly fine. A healthy, normal red-blooded 'honey-gettin' man who ain't passing up free cookies in this life or the next," laughs Ty high-fiving Carlos again.

"You better watch yourself man, you're getting too old for all that," Eddie advises. "Might catch something that you can't get rid of in that cookie jar!" Charles points his finger in Eddie's direction giving him the 'you right' nod of agreement.

"Eddie how long you been married, man?" Inquires Ty.

"Priscilla and I are coming up on our 8th anniversary in June." States Eddie proudly.

"Ok, enough said. I rest my case," says Ty.

"You've obviously gotten use to stale cookies!" Ty finishes to the roar of laughter of the men in the room.

"That's alright, man," defends Eddie, calm and collected.

"The cookies are mine exclusively and only eaten by me." He continues. "Know you can't say the same fresh Cookie Man!" Eddie shoots back with a slick smile, not taking his eyes off the cards in his hand.

"Every last one of you needs Jesus!" Interjects Charles, moving a king of hearts to the center of the trio of cards he has left in his hands.

"Oh man, don't start with the preaching!"

"I love me some Jesus; and some honeys too!" The good Lord knows my heart." Ty says placing his free hand over his chest feigning humility.

"Yeah, that's the problem," offers Eddie, re-shuffling the deck in preparation for the next round.

The night with the boys rolls on with all of its usual and expected jokes, anecdotes and antics. Around 2 am, Charles plays his last hand and bids adieu to his buddies. Zipping his jacket and heading out of Ty's apartment, he greets the cool of the late night, early morning. Instantly rejuvenated, Charles moves in an easy gait to his waiting car with thoughts of Deirdre dancing across his mind. He tries to resist the urge to call her in the middle of the night, but is overcome by a stronger need to make contact with her. He sends a text.

"Hey, baby. Thinking of you."

Deirdre up herself entertaining her own thoughts of Charles while attempting to finish a novel that she's been reading for months; smiles when she hears her phone signal a message received. Knowingly, she reaches over to the nightstand next to her bed and retrieves the phone.

"Me too." Deirdre texts back.

"What r u doing?" Charles texts back.

"Reading. You?"

"Falling in Love" Charles texts back again.

"Me too." Deirdre responds, shutting off the phone and laying her book on top of the small pile of books next to her bed. She reaches for the light next to the silenced phone, turns it off as well and finally pursues the bliss of a long awaited good night's sleep. Smiling with a sense of relief, Charles texts back a "smile" and shuts off his phone for the rest of the drive home in the sanctuary of his solitude.

" Love is stronger than death, my brother. Choose wisely."
--Pastor Chuck

A couple of weeks later …

The two men, one young the other older settle into an empty booth in the bustling local diner. Looking like father and son, they draw the attention of a hostess who gingerly moves around the counter that separates her from incoming patrons to greet them with menus in tow.

"Good morning , gentleman your waitress will be right with you, momentarily. Can I get you a cup of coffee while you wait?" she asks in a friendly, but obviously rehearsed tone.

"No, thank you," the men answer almost in unison.

"We're ready to order. We'll have coffee after our meal." The older of the two informs the hostess. Turning his closely cropped distinguished silver-gray head fully back to Charles he smiles gently, glad to see the younger man.

"Glad that you could make it Uncle Pete," starts Charles a little nervously. Uncle Pete always had a way of making him overly self conscious about the way that he presented himself. The discomfort would quickly subside within moments of their conversations; but the first few words that came out of his mouth in discussions with Uncle Pete were intentionally guarded. Uncle Pete had a way of making young men feel the urge to straighten their backs and ties, if they wore one and look him directly in the eye when they spoke to him. Although no longer the strapping young man of his yesteryears, his very presence still commanded respect.

"Since when have I ever not accepted an invitation to a free breakfast especially when you're paying." Joust the older man with a mischievous twinkle in his eyes.

"But I know that you didn't ask me to meet you just to eat some overpriced English muffins and eggs together.
What's on your mind, son?" With a hesitant start, Charles jumps right into the reason why he needed to talk to the older man in person today.

"Well, you know that I am seeing an older woman?"

"Yes son, the young lady with the teenage son, right?"

"Right."

"Yes, how are things going between the two of you? It's been a couple of months now, I believe?"

"Yes, sir." Responds Charles. "8 weeks to be exact. If anyone is counting."

"Well, it appears that you are, son. Everything o.k.?"

"Well, yes and no, sir. You see, I think that she is the woman for me and I have no issues with the fact that she is 10 years older and already has a child from a previous marriage. But by the same token, I want to have kids with the woman I eventually marry…"

"Whoa, marriage son? So soon?"

"Well, yes and no, sir."

"Son, that's the second time in 10 minutes that you've given me the 'yes and no, sir' response."

"Good morning, what can I get for you two handsome young men today?, " greets a middle-aged blonde with green notepad and pencil in hand.

"What's going on, Charles?" asks the older man initially ignoring the waiting waitress to finish his comments.

"Good morning, beautiful," says Uncle Pete briefly pausing to look up at the inquiring woman. Returning his fixed gazed on Charles' unsettled countenance, he says to the waitress, "Why don't you bring us both an order of sunny side up eggs, toast and English muffins, with a side order of sausage and bacon."

"Sure thing," responds the waitress as she swiftly lifts the menus off the Formica table and returns them to the front of the restaurant.

"Uncle Pete, I know that we just met, but I feel like I've known Deirdre forever. When I am with her and Tommy I feel complete, like I have the family that I've always craved. Ty was right about her being a little bitter, but I understand why she is the way that she is. She's really an easygoing person once you cut through the walls that she has placed around her heart to protect herself. I understand it and there is ...," abruptly interrupting himself, Charles lunges into the inevitable.

"Uncle Pete have you ever been in a relationship with a woman who you just felt like covering, protecting, and providing for? A woman who you felt that you could get close enough to in time to love like Christ loves the church?" he finishes nearly exhausted from the sudden rush of adrenalin.

"You mean a woman who you would sacrifice your very life for, son?"

"I guess that's a stupid question." Charles says reflectively and visibly calmer.

"You have Alicia and she seems to be making you very happy as a wife," he continues.

"Ah, yes my lovely young bride is indeed the apple of my eye. But let me tell you something man to man, son. Alicia may very well be the last woman that I love like that; but she certainly is not the first." The older gentleman replies with a firmness that suits his regal demeanor. "In fact, from the things that you have told me about this new love interest of yours over the last several weeks, in many ways, I mean in more ways than one, she reminds me of a single mother that I was sweet on some 30 years ago. Headstrong, independent and self-directed."

"My mother, right?"

"Who else, son?"

"Uncle Pete can I ask you a personal question?"

"Son, you know that you can ask me anything."

"Why didn't you and my mother ever marry each other?"

"Boy you've been asking that personal question for 28 years!" the older man slowly grins and chuckles lightly.

"If I recall, you first asked me that same question on your 10th birthday. I took you out to a ballgame and you told me how you wished that I could be your real father, since you didn't have one that you knew. And why couldn't your mother and I just get married and make it easier on everybody?" the old man smiles as he reminisces.

"It doesn't take much to start a fight son, any fool can do that. But it takes the strength of a wise man to know when to fight; and when to hold his peace."

--Pastor Elijah Mordecai Smith

Early autumn, a couple of months later...

It's early Saturday morning and Tommy is on his third bowl of Captain Munch. "Tommy watch what you're doing. You're about to spill cereal all over the place," warns Deirdre as her son continues to pour too much milk in a bowl teaming with mini multi-colored squares.

"Oh, snap!" Tommy exclaims as the contents of the bowl overflows onto the table as predicted. Deirdre shakes her head and sighs moving toward the sink to grab a sponge and paper towels for the clean up.

"Sorry 'bout that, Mom." Tommy offers sheepishly.

"Boy, if you would just listen. Your head is as hard as granite."

"Granite? Hey, I learned about that in Science last year!" The teen proudly announces.

"Isn't that the hardest substance known to mankind?" he asks slightly bewildered by the comparison.

"My point exactly." Deirdre says finishing the cereal clean up and returning the sponge and paper towels to the kitchen counter.

"So, Mom are we hanging out with Charles tonight?" earnestly inquires Tommy equally anxious to know and to change the subject.

"He finally beat me after a dozen tries on that game that he gave me. I will not be defeated by an old guy! This is war!" declares Tommy with a raised cereal spoon in the air dripping milk.

"Um, Mr. Video Game Warrior, you're about to make another mess." Informs Deirdre rolling her eyes heaven ward and moving away from the breakfast table toward her ringing phone in the next room.

"Hey, Baby. What you up to?" says Charles on the other end.

"Not much today. Tommy and I are just finishing up breakfast. He's hanging out with my cousin and her kids this afternoon for her son's birthday party. Other than that, I'm free."

"Why? What's up?

"Nothing much. Just need to run over to the Paint Depo." Says Charles. "The garage needs a fresh coat. Wanna' run with me today?" He asks.

"Oh, thought you were going to ask me to help you paint." Deirdre laughs.

"And you would say yes to that too, right my Lovely Lady?"

"Wrong, Sir."

"I will happily go with you to buy the paint and gleefully sit and watch you as you do the painting!" Deirdre jokes.

"Oh, so it's like that?"

"Yep."

"Well it looks like I have to take what I can get , because I want to see you."

"Charles, we just saw each other 2 nights ago."

"I know. But that was 48 hours ago," he clowns.

"You so silly!" Says Deirdre laughing again. "Ok, pick me up in an hour."

"Deirdre, please be ready."

"Ok, I promise this time I won't keep you waiting."

"Oh, remember that we have that dinner party at my cousin's house tonight."

"Right. Formal affair?"

"No, no. Just wear what you normally wear when you and I go out to dinner." Says Charles. "Believe me, that'll be just fine," he adds suggestively.

"You need Jesus!" Deirdre says using his often used reprimand back on him.

"Yep. Sure do. So, glad I have Him." Admits Charles unashamedly.

"Mom, was that Charles?" asks Tommy waiting expectantly for an answer.

"Yes it was, Mister."

"So, are we going over to his house tonight? I've got beef with him that must be settled man to man," Tommy asserts.

"Lord child! What am I going to do with you?" Deirdre chuckles playfully mussing up his close cropped hair.

"The waves, Mom! The waves! You're messing up my waves!" Tommy says ducking to protect his latest teenage boy-do.

"Oh boy, Please!" says Deirdre heading to the bathroom to jump in the shower.

"Mom, you never answered me. Are we hanging with Charles tonight? I really need to know."

"I am, Tommy, but you're not."

"Awwh, man!"

"You have Dickey's birthday party this afternoon, remember?"

"Oh, yeah! I forgot." The teen quickly recovers.

"Am I sleeping over?" He asks.

"Yeah, Cousin Sheila will bring you to church in the morning. I'll meet you there."

"Yes!" The teen pumps his fist in the air.

"Was that for the sleepover or meeting me in church tomorrow morning?" Deirdre shouts out to the teen over the roar of the shower with a hint of sarcasm. Tommy who has planted himself immediately outside of the closed bathroom door responds,

"It was for meeting you in church my dear mother, of course," he says returning the sarcasm in his best imitation of a well-spoken gentleman before walking away from the door into his bedroom.

"Don't turn on that game system until you get that room cleaned, Tommy!" Deirdre shouts one last time from the bathroom.

"Dag!" Tommy pouts putting down the game controller that he just picked up.

Saturday evening, After 5...

"So where does your cousin live?" asks Deirdre comfortably in the passenger seat of Charles' car searching through his mini stack of CD's.

"Ernest and his wife Marva live a few miles north of here, just up the Parkway a bit. It's a 20 minute drive tops, even in traffic. Not far. We'll be there sooner than you can decide which CD to put in," Charles teases.

"Hmmm, 20 minutes north on the Parkway? Your cousin must have some money?"

"Actually he has quite a bit and he makes it his business to make sure that everyone knows it." Chuckles Charles.

"I should warn you; Ernest is a bit of a jerk. Always has been, even before he became rich. Please whatever you do, don't take him too seriously." Charles adds.

"No one in the family does. He's just being Ernest Wilmore Monroe. Never understood how Uncle Julius who was probably one of the coolest dudes alive; could have a son like Ernest. It just never made sense to me even when we were kids." Charles reflects.

"Believe me, I've spent enough time in the corporate world to learn how to manage my fair share of jerks." Deirdre says reassuringly.

"Good." Says Charles. "Because he's family and you're my heart. Just don't want you to get offended by something that most of us are pretty use to by now." Sincerely states Charles.

"Well, with that warning, I better put on something to pre-condition my nerves." Deirdre says laughing lightly as she finally makes a music selection and pops it into the player.

"Oh, Jean Carne! That's what I'm talking about! Some Old School R&B!" Deirdre proclaims with genuine excitement.

"Don't let it go to your head, boy!" Deirdre sings along snapping her fingers in the air. Charles momentarily takes his eyes off the road and glances over at the singing and dancing woman next to him and smiles.

"Don't let it , Don't let it, Don't let it! Go! To your head boy!"
Deirdre teasingly sings directly to Charles pointing to his head.

"Too late." Charles gently responds, still smiling at Deirdre's antics with his attention fully turned back to the road.

"Nice neighborhood." Deirdre comments a few seconds after Charles exits the Parkway and drives along tree lined streets with homes that seemingly increase in size by every fraction of a mile. No more than a few minutes and another mile or two transpire before they come to a final winding road that has about a half dozen homes that sit a least a half of a football field in distance from the non-existing curbs.

"Wow! You weren't kidding when you said your cousin was loaded." Deirdre notes slightly taken aback by the immensity of the property that they just turned into off of a lush country road.

"What does your cousin do?" She curiously asks.

"He started a small technology firm right out of Harvard Business School that took off; and with the exception of only a few setbacks over the years, never stopped growing." Charles continues, "He seemed to have the knack for staying on the cutting-edge of new technologies and always made the right moves at the right time; well most of the time," he adds. Remembering something that he chooses not to share. "And despite his annoying attitudes and behaviors; I am secretly really proud of him. Of course, I never tell him that. It would just go to his already inflated, outsized ego," says Charles conspiratorially moving in closer to Deirdre as if someone else can hear him.

"Did I tell you how good you look tonight, baby?" Charles adds taking advantage of the proximity between him and Deirdre before getting out of the car.

"Yes, you have, Mr. Monroe." Deirdre says playfully touching the tip of his nose.

"Well, I think it needs to be said again." He says gently lifting her chin. "Like this." He whispers kissing her softly.
Gently releasing his embrace he smiles and lingers for a moment before being interrupted by a tap on the driver's side window.

"Good Evening, Mr. Monroe. Would you like for me to park your car for you tonight?"

"Hey, Josh," greets Charles. "No thanks, he continues peering up and out of his partially rolled down car window to speak to the young valet.

"I'll just pull up in my regular spot. Just in case we decide to leave early." He says.

"No problem, sir. Have a good evening," says the younger man.

"Thanks," says Charles and proceeds to swing his sedan around to a familiar spot immediately behind a late model Mercedes.

"Charles, I really wasn't expecting all of this," says Deirdre growing a little uneasy as he helps her out of the car.

"Oh, you haven't seen anything, yet. Wait until you get inside." Charles offers with intrigue. "Ernest Wilmore Monroe is 'The Host with the Most'." Charles jokes in attempt to make Deirdre feel a sense of comfort that simply escapes her at the moment. She recalled traveling home with some of her college buddies on occasion who lived in some pretty palatial houses; but nothing compared to the property that she was currently standing on. Briefly lost in her thoughts, Deirdre snaps herself back into the present reality. Shaking off the sudden onslaught of negative emotions; she takes a deep breath, squares her shoulders, lifts her chin and smiles back at Charles as they walk hand in hand toward the entrance of his cousin's mansion.

"Well, well, well, if it isn't my peculiar cousin Charles," smirks Ernest upon Charles and Deirdre's entry into the large reception area of the vast Great Room that is comfortably accommodating about a dozen well-dressed cocktail sipping dinner guests.

"Hey Ernest. How are you, man?"
Sincerely responds Charles grabbing his cousin's hand and pulling him to himself in a man hug.

"And to whom do I owe the pleasure of having this lovely lady in my home tonight?" greets Ernest moving out of his cousin's embrace to extend a hand to Deirdre.

"Ernest meet Deirdre Parker, the love of my life," says Charles to Deirdre's complete surprise.

"Nice to meet you Ernest," says Deirdre casting a wary eye Charles' way.

"Hmmmm, always admired your taste in women, Charles." Says Ernest speaking to Charles without taking his eyes off Deirdre.

"Indeed."

He adds smiling at Deirdre as his wife approaches their little circle of three.

"Good evening, I'm Marva Monroe. So, nice to meet you. You must be Deirdre Parker? " The tall attractive woman says extending a slender manicured hand with a diamond that matches the sparkling drop earrings that seem to follow the slightest tilt of her head.

"Yes, nice to meet you as well." Says Deirdre moving just a few steps ahead of the two men with the hostess into the larger area.

"Not bad, cuz. Not bad at all." Assesses Ernest as they both watch the women walking ahead of them.

"Does she know that you are a garbage man?" asks Ernest in all seriousness.

"Yes, she knows that and a lot of other stuff about me, man. And it's all good." Charles says slapping his cousin on the back for affirmation as he walks away from him to catch up with the women.

"Oh, Charles, darling how are you?" Says Marva interrupting herself in mid sentence. Turning briefly away from Deirdre she continues, "I didn't greet you properly! Shame on me!" smiles

Marva grabbing both of Charles hands and placing a feather light kiss on his cheek.

"Hey, Marva. Always good to see you." Says Charles.

"You look lovely as usual," he says stepping back to admire the hostess.

"So, Ms. Parker what do you do?" Says Ernest now standing alone alongside Deirdre and picking up his conversation with her once again as Marva and Charles exchange pleasantries.

"I am a former Wall Streeter. I managed mutual funds for an investment house that specialized in non-profit agency portfolios. Had to pack it in with most when the roof caved in. I was on that first wave of recession restructuring," shares Deirdre.

"Ah, yes. Maintaining wealth in this current economy can be a challenge, for some." Airily states Ernest.

"Who can forget the historic lows of the market over the past few years?" Asks Ernest not really wanting or waiting for an answer. He continues, "My portfolio took quite a hit as well," he offers in mock disgust. "Who enjoys losing money? After all, we're in business to make money!" Ernest emphatically adds and continues his questioning.

"So, what is your present line of work?"

"I am a Community Liaison for East River Savings & Trust and work out of the Jersey City headquarters," says Deirdre unconsciously looking in Charles direction hoping that he will soon return to her side.

"Sounds like you landed on your feet," comments Ernest.

"It's a good job and I am good at it. But it is in no way comparable to Wall Street."

"I see you two have found quite a lot to talk about." Interjects Marva protectively moving next to her husband and interlocking her slender arm around his.

"Indeed, Ms. Parker and I were just trading war stories about the market." Ernest says smiling down at his wife.

"Well, let's go into the dining room, I believe Louis is ready to serve the evening meal." Says Marva leading the way to an ornate room with multiple chandeliers and an enormous antique dining table at its center elaborately set for 12.

"Charles did I ever tell you how I stole Louis from the Four Seasons in Philadelphia?" Says Ernest turning to Charles as his wife makes introductions around the table and directs Deirdre and Charles to seats next to them near the head of the table where Ernest settles in and continues his story.

"Marva and I went to Philly to catch the closing performance of the Philadelphia Philharmonic for one of her annual charity events and stayed at the Four Seasons." He pauses to sip a crystal glass of white wine.

"Louis was the Head Chef and prepared a mean filet mignon. Hired him on the spot!" Ernest brags.

"Brings new meaning to ordering take out!" chimes in one of the dinner guest sitting within earshot of the conversation.

"I'd say," adds another at the table. Everyone chuckles as light chatter continues among the diners, glasses clink and appetizers are consumed. As the evening slowly unfolds, Deirdre quickly comes to the conclusion that Ernest's little dinner parties are self-serving opportunities for displaying his wealth and stroking his ego. King of the heap, holding court from the throne-like chair at the head of his king-sized dining table with all of his little minions around him. His anecdotes and jokes are increasingly less humorous as the evening progresses. Although most of his guests chuckle and smile on cue showing no outward signs of having had enough; Deirdre is getting annoyed and antsy. Even Charles' display of tolerance toward his cousin quickly became a point of contention for her. Despite the fact that she initially thought it noble of him to put up with such nonsense. Now, however, she is grossly irritated by the whole ordeal that someone is calling a dinner party.

"So, Ms. Parker, I don't recall you mentioning where you matriculated?" States Ernest halfway through dinner and after about a bottle and a half of Chablis of which he consumed the lion's share.

"Ah, no. As a matter of fact, I didn't." Says Deirdre with just enough of an edge to keep Ernest off of her. Relentless in his pursuit of something intangible, he continues,

"You remind me a lot of the Radcliffe women that I went to school with."

"I am a Beecher College graduate."

"Ah, no surprise there." Says Ernest nodding his head in agreement with himself. "Excellent school," he adds.

"My roommate's sister was a Beecher girl. But you seem a wee bit older; you were probably already on Wall Street by then." Ernest says with an oblique smile looking directly at Deirdre to register the effect of his dig. Charles clears his throat as he protectively places his hand on top of Deirdre's.

"Ernest, have you talked to Uncle Jack since putting him in the nursing home?" Ernest momentarily thrown off-guard by Charles' interception, recovers quickly and responds,

"As a matter of fact, Marva just returned from Savannah earlier this week and made a quick stop-over in Beaufort to check on Uncle Jack." Clearing his throat and grabbing a pristine white linen napkin, Ernest continues as he dabs the corners of his mouth and returns the cloth to the table.

"He's in the best facility that the state has to offer. I spared no expense." He says allowing his eyes to challenge the intensity of Charles' countenance.

"After all he is the last of my father's brothers; the eldest and the only Monroe brother out of the five still alive."

He finishes again with a half smile.

"How are things at the Sanitation Department, Charles," asks Ernest smoothly changing the subject and raising a few eyebrows at the table. Before Charles can respond, Ernest continues.

"What is it 20 years or more that you've been there, man? You should be running the place by now," derisively laughs Ernest. Deirdre's brown face flushes anger that she attempts to control, but unconsciously slams her wine glass down on the table spilling just enough to warrant a quick change of service by the attendant who instantly appears at her side. Charles fully aware of the impact that his cousin is having on Deirdre, excuses both himself and Deirdre from the table.

"Excuse us, please. I think we're both wearing quite a bit of Chablis right now," says Charles politely to Ernest and his guests as he and Deirdre are escorted by the head servant to the guest suite. Facing Charles as soon as they are left alone in the well-appointed room Deirdre lashes out in a whispered shout,

"What in the hell is wrong with your cousin?"

Enraged, she continues, "What an idiot! Who does he think he is?" She angrily declares.

"Look baby, Ernest is a jerk. He's always been a jerk. He was a jerk before he became rich; even when we were kids running around our parents' backyards together. And he is still a jerk with estate property, a fleet of luxury cars, pretty wife and all!" Taking a deep breath and squaring Deirdre's face and shoulders in front of him, Charles continues to speak.

"I've learned to ignore his antics since childhood. Please try to do the same. He's family."

"Ignore him?" Deirdre questions incredulously.

"He's rude, Charles. He's a rude-ass man!" She exclaims shrilly and visibly upset. "I can't and won't ignore him." She indignantly declares. "Trust me, I've encountered some real mean-spirited folks in the workplace, but you don't act this way with family, Charles. Come on! This is ridiculous!"

"Ok, Deirdre. So what do you want me to do?" Sighs Charles.

"Can we leave? I really can't take anymore of this." Deirdre confesses. "I've had enough."

"Baby, can we at least finish the meal?" Charles pleas with Deirdre who is beginning to regain her composure to some degree.

"Yes, but please let's get out of here as soon as dinner is over."

"Ok," concedes Charles placing a light kiss on Deirdre's forehead as he takes her hand in his and leads her out of the room toward the sound of light banter, clinking wine glasses and unfettered consumption.

About an hour and a-half later…

"Whew, glad that's over!" Deirdre confesses as she settles into the passenger seat of Charles' car and buckles up.

"You ok?" Asks Charles with genuine concern.

"Yep. It actually wasn't so bad." Deirdre responds wearily.

"There's something good underneath all of Ernest's bravado; can't quite put my finger on it; but he seems salvageable."

"Because he is." Informs Charles.

"The problem with my cousin is that he absolutely does not factor God into anything that he is or does. He has turned his back on the very values that our upbringing has stood on for generations. Love of God, protection and care of family and old-fashioned hard work; in that order. He continues, "Ernest thinks his wealth has come by his own hand and ingenuity; and has even said so. 'My power and the strength of my own mind and willingness to work hard have gained me this wealth' " Charles says doing a convincing imitation of his cousin.

"He's forgotten God. He doesn't remember that it is the Lord who gave him power to get wealth. The last time Ernest even stepped foot in a church was when we funeralized his father, my uncle Julius. That was more that 15 years ago, and he hasn't been in anyone's church since." Shares Charles. "But he is family and I love him despite his idiosyncrasies."

Deirdre gently shuts her front door with a light sigh and climbs the single flight of stairs to her apartment, which feels even smaller after having spent the last 3 hours of the evening in a mansion. Usually not one to compare herself to others, particularly with regard to material trappings; she registers a slight discontent as she steps into her bedroom which is literally smaller than the guest bathroom of the Monroe mansion. Peeling off the support pantyhose that successfully held her hips and thighs captive throughout the evening; Deirdre undresses slowly, completely engrossed in thought.

Moving toward the bathroom, she peers into the mirror and audibly asks herself, "Girl, what in the world are you doing?" Sighing again as she grabs cold cream to remove her after 5 make-up in preparation for a much needed good night's sleep. "You're 48 years old with a teenage son and a ½ college educated, 38 year old boyfriend who picks up garbage for a living." Her thoughts stream into her head unfiltered. "A man who also makes me cry when he kisses me goodnight; and melts down every defense that I can muster," she whispers aloud to herself as she clicks off her bedroom lamplight and pulls her comforter securely over her quaking shoulders.

Charles didn't make it to church, so Deirdre sat on their favorite pew alone wondering if last night's comedy of errors at his cousin's encouraged his absence this Sunday morning. Tommy who tucked himself away in the balcony with his cousin Dickey and a whole host of other teens, didn't meet up with Deirdre until after the service. She was alone, again; and somewhat relieved by her solitary state.

Being alone today allowed her to cry freely throughout the worship service. At first it was a particular worship song, then it was a scripture read from her favorite book of the Bible. The final blow was Pastor Chuck's sermon. Was he at her house last night when she cried herself to sleep? How did his spoken words so connect with exactly what she was going through, feeling, thinking, struggling with?

"We always look at Ruth's blessing in being found by Boaz. How about Boaz' blessing? The Bible teaches that 'He who finds a wife finds a good thing!' " Fervently declares the robed gentleman. "Boaz wasn't a young man, but God blessed him with a young wife late in life." The preacher pauses briefly to make his point. "Listen to me my single brothers and sisters. Hear me!" He commands while wiping his brow with a handkerchief that seems to appear out of nowhere. "Some of you are passing up your blessings because you're caught up on things that really shouldn't matter if you are truly in Christ." The Reverend continues, "If you are primarily concerned with age, race and social economic status; Oh please! You'll live a lonely solitary life. No, I'm sorry. I'm wrong for saying that," the clergyman retracts. "You have Jesus; but what you won't have is something that He Himself might want to give you in this earthly life; true love and real Godly companionship." Winding down to a close, he implores, "Take off the limitations. Take God out of the box! He's too big a God to be limited by our human limitations. Doesn't matter how late in life love comes; or the color, shape or size it comes, as long as it comes from the Father; it's always good and worth the wait," he finishes to more than a few Amens as he gestures to the congregation to stand for the call to Discipleship and the Benediction.

Rising to her feet, Deirdre reaches again for another tissue and dabs her moist eyes.

Outside of the church and headed for the adjacent parking lot, she turns on her phone to give Charles a call.

"Hey Love," Charles answers after a few short rings.

"Did you get my text?" He inquires.

"No, I just got out of church. Haven't checked messages yet." Deirdre says finally spotting Tommy who is headed in her direction with a trio of balcony buddies and his cousin.

"What happened to you today? Too much Monroe-mania last night?" Deirdre half-jokingly asks.

"Very funny, Dee," responds Charles not finding much humor in either her statement nor the events of yesterday evening. Moving on, he states, "Actually, a colleague of mine was hospitalized last night; so I decided to spend the morning visiting him."

"Oh, sorry to hear that." Says Deirdre.

"I hope that he's going to be ok." She adds sincerely.

"Willie is as strong as an ox. He'll be alright." Changing the subject, Charles asks, "So, what are you up to for the rest of the day?"

"Nothing much. Guess I'll go home, make dinner and try to relax for a few hours until time to prepare for work tomorrow."

"Why not have dinner with me? Charles suggests.

"Tell Tommy to bring his best game," he laughs.

"No, not tonight, Charles. I'm really exhausted. Plus, I need to get Tommy settled in and ready for the week ahead. I'm sure there's some homework assignment lurking in that backpack of his that needs attention tonight." Deirdre offers by way of excuse. Charles sensing something more than fatigue and the call of motherly duty hindering Deirdre's desire, let's her off the hook.

"Ok, baby. Perhaps we'll get together one evening this week."

"Of course."

Responds Deirdre unsure of why she isn't so sure anymore.

"Dee, I love you." Gently states Charles before releasing the line.

"Me too," responds Deirdre before hanging up.

It was the second consecutive Sunday that Deirdre did not show up for Church. Charles sat alone in a crowd on the back pew wondering what was going on. She wasn't returning calls as frequently and even declined Charles' usual offer to take Tommy to basketball practice so that she could have some time to herself. Something she always seemed to look forward to at least a couple of evenings a week. Charles' generosity also gave them all more time to hangout together in the evening hours and share a meal or late night snack either at his place or hers.

"Good morning, Mother Clarke," Charles says settling down in the pew directly behind the elderly woman.

"Hey, Sugar. How are you this morning, Baby? Where's that nice girl ya' dating today? What's her name? Dee Dee?"

"Deirdre, Mam."

"Right, right. You two make a beautiful couple." Offers Mrs. Clarke with her signature smile.

"Thank you, Mother Clarke."

"So when are you going to ask her to marry you, son?" Mother Clarke continues. "You know, my beloved Henry, God bless his soul, proposed to me right here in this sanctuary in front of the whole Church in 1946. It was a year after the war ended. I knew my Henry loved me; but I didn't know just how much until he came in here all dressed up fine and handsome in his uniform with the biggest diamond ring I had ever seen in my life! When Pastor Elijah

Mordecai Smith called him up in front of the Church that Sunday morning, I didn't think anything of it. My Henry being the good Christian soldier that he was; Pastor could have called him up for any reason. But Lord have mercy! That Sunday my Henry gets up and leaves my side to go up to the altar with Pastor Elijah loomin' large over and above him from the pulpit looking like Frederick Douglass with all of that wild salt and pepper hair he had back then for such a young man!" The older woman chuckles and continues. "I declare, I don't know what set the devil a flight more, that man's praying or that hair!" Laughs Mother Clarke showing all of her dentured teeth. "Well, he called my Henry up front and lo and behold Pastor calls me too! Well chile, you could have knocked my 17 year old self over with a feather! I was done! Henry proposed to me right here at Mt. Moriah in May of 1946 almost a year to the day that he returned home from the war in Germany. Yes, indeed," the elderly woman reminisces.

"Him in his uniform looking all handsome and sharp and me in my Sunday Best smiling from ear to ear! Bless the Lord, chile. God is so good! We got married that June and lived 60 happily married years together until the Good Lord called my Henry home 3 years ago." Mother Clarke suddenly becomes quiet and pensive.

"Lord knows I miss my Henry; but I know I'll see him again in heaven one day soon," the elderly woman finishes on a hopeful note.

"Well, not too soon Mother Clarke, because we need you here with us!" Encourages Charles giving the elder woman a gentle hug.

About 2 hours later…

Charles rises from his seat at the conclusion of the worship service. Taking a moment to say goodbye to Mother Clarke, he exits the sanctuary preoccupied with thoughts of Deirdre. His first impulse is to go to her house unannounced and confront the situation head on. She was obviously avoiding him. But why? Frustrated and angry; Charles gets in his car and heads home without another thought about or word from Deirdre. His success in pushing her out of his mind lasted through the first half of the 2nd game. That's when the lack of activity, chatter and laughter in his home on a Sunday afternoon jettisoned his thoughts right back to the absence of Deirdre and Tommy.

Sundays had become particularly special for Charles, Deirdre and Tommy. They spent the entire day together from morning to evening. Church service, brunch afterwards and evening dinner time filled with good natured teasing, laughter, and interesting conversation. Good company. Charles loved Deirdre and Tommy; they were now a significant part of his life; like family. He thought she felt the same way about him. So why the avoidance game?

By early evening, Charles had had enough. Hauling his well-built frame from the leather couch that he'd been parked on all afternoon; he clicked the remote and watched the large TV screen go black. The silence was deafening. In the stillness of the early evening, Charles lost in his thoughts just stared at the blank screen feeling an emptiness that he hadn't felt since childhood. Sitting back down, he reached for his phone among discarded fast food containers , soda cans and the sports section of the Sunday newspaper on the coffee table in front of him and called Deirdre.

"Hi, Charles." Deirdre meekly answered her phone after a long series of rings.

"Deirdre, we need to talk," says Charles, skipping the preliminaries.

"Sure, come on over," responds Deirdre.

"I'm on my way," states Charles releasing the line, again without a closing salutation. Feeling the discomfort of a pending storm, Deirdre also releases her line with a heaviness of heart.

"Lord, give me strength," she whispers to herself as she attempts to prepare for the inevitable. Less than 10 minutes later her doorbell rings. Thankful that Tommy is not yet home from his weekend visit with his father, Deirdre quickly tidies up her immediate surroundings picking up unopened mail on the floor and a few carelessly discarded shoes and clothing items around her small apartment.

"Hey," she says opening her front door and letting Charles in.

"Hey baby," Charles says taking Dee in fully before moving past her and up the short flight of stairs to her abode. Once comfortably seated on her overstuffed couch, Charles again seeming to meditate on the composition of her demeanor asks,

"What's going on, Dee?"

"Nothing, Charles. I've just been really busy with work and all." She offers knowing that she's only telling a half-truth.

"Deirdre, let's not play games with each other. You have been avoiding me for weeks. In fact, things haven't been the same between us since we went to Ernest's house. Why?" Charles firmly questions waiting for an answer that Deirdre struggles to give.

"I don't know, Charles." Deirdre begins.

"I just don't know if we are really right for each other." She hesitates before continuing, dropping her eyes to avoid the pools of pain that her words elicit in the eyes of the man sitting directly across from her.

"I don't know," she nervously continues, repeating herself and fidgeting with a link in a tennis bracelet; a recent gift from Charles.

"I know," says Charles rising from the couch opposite the one Deirdre is perched on and plants himself directly in front of her on bended knee. Waiting for Deirdre's eyes to meet his Charles continues, "Can't you see that you're fighting destiny, Deirdre?" Charles asks exasperated.

"You can come up with a thousand reasons why we shouldn't be together, but there's only one reason that's controlling you and that's fear." He pauses, looking intensely into to Deirdre's eyes. "We were made for each other, Dee. It's not about how old you are and how young I am ... it's about what we've been through and learned in life... and believe me, I've learned a lot from all that I've been through."

Placing his hands on her trembling shoulders, Charles releases one hand to gently lift Deirdre's chin and tear stained profile turning her face again in his direction. Waiting patiently for their eyes to meet, he continues,

"Listen Deirdre, We've both been through a lot. But let me tell you the single most important thing that I've learned through it all, is how to truly love. I know that love is kind, it's not selfish, doesn't always have to have things its way or the highway, it's gentle, it listens, it serves, it protects, it fights for what is right ...and I know that you know and believe that too," he finishes rising to leave.

Deirdre unable to respond looks up and into Charles' pleading eyes. Wiping tears that have quietly escaped, she also rises almost meeting Charles eye to eye. Now looking up at him once again from a standing position, she finally finds the courage to speak.

"Charles, it's over between you and I." She swallows hard and continues. "It's not just our age difference, but a lot of other really complicated things too hard to explain. Things that I just can't put into words that'll make sense to you or even myself." Without another word Charles gently caresses Deirdre's tear stained face and draws her to himself. He kisses her tenderly. In the silence that ensues he releases her and moves toward the stairs to leave her house and her presence.

"Deirdre." Charles says finally breaking the prolonged silence once he reaches the front door. "As long as God blesses me with breath in my body, I'm not giving up on you or us. Ever." Declares Charles in a frustrated whisper before moving through the door into the night.

A gentle evening breeze greets him just as he steps off the porch onto the short walkway leading to his car. The wind blows a second time lightly over his shoulders as he pauses momentarily and looks up briefly at the night sky and then continues to his parked vehicle, gets in and drives away …

Once home Charles attempts for the second time in a day to take his mind off Deirdre and all that has transpired between him and the woman that he loves from a place so deep within that he cannot fully comprehend. After a number of failed attempts to shift his thoughts he surrenders; shuts off the TV and heads to his bedroom hoping to find relief and a modicum of comfort in sleep. Mentally exhausted and emotionally spent, Charles strips down to his boxers and falls back on his bed, with arms and hands behind his head, face-up and staring at the ceiling. As the war of his emotions prevails he does the only thing that he's ever known to do to stop the warfare.

He prays. Kneeling down at his bedside, Charles prays to God asking for wisdom in his relationship with Deirdre and for his life.

"Lord. I don't even know what to say. How many times have I asked you to fix things for me and again and again and you come through for me every time... Father God, I first want to thank you for your faithfulness to me down through the years. You say in your Word that you are a Father to the Fatherless and I am living proof that your Word is true. You've made me the man that I am today by sending so many Godly men and women my way to help me grow up and mature and teach me how to be a real man. Now I believe that you have sent me a real woman who I believe that I can love the way that you want a man to love his wife. Actually, Lord, I know that I love Deirdre the way that Christ loves the Church. I would give my very life for her. But I don't want to die for her, I want to live to love her like you love... with your love. And I promise you , Lord, I'll love her until the day that I die."

Charles, lingers, silent for a moment taking in his own words spoken to an unseen, but strongly felt God. He continues,

"I don't know why things have gotten so hard between us. But I trust you to work all things together for our good. You are in control, Lord God. I trust you. We've broken down so many walls... but it feels like we still have something to overcome... help us Lord. Help me to make the right

choices and decisions. Show me, give me another sign that Deirdre is the woman who you have chosen just for me."

He closes his conversation wanting to make the right choices. He wants what he wants really badly, more than anything... but the only thing he wants more than his own will is the will of God for his life. Later in the same week, he finds himself in church Sunday morning at the altar, making the same prayer request to the LORD, once again.

Charles moves on, respecting Deirdre's request that they not see each other anymore. He neither calls, texts or attempts to initiate any contact with her. She and Tommy leave Mt. Moriah. According to one of the many women that Ty dated from time to time, she joined a big church in the next county over.

"Son, one day you are going to need a strength and a power that will reach your highest mountains and flow through your lowest valleys. And quite frankly, I haven't found any greater than the humble Jewish carpenter from Galilee."

--Uncle Pete

To the undiscerning eye, Charles had succeeded in outwardly moving on without Dee. Yet, his soul ties to her were more tenacious than he could have ever imagined. Most days he could navigate the emotional turmoil running in the background of his heart and make it through the day without feeling the loss. But like the grief that comes with death, it crept up on him at the most inopportune and vulnerable times. While simply driving along listening to the radio to keep his mind in neutral a song would come on that he and Dee use to clown around to and sing Karaoke style while driving around town running errands on a Saturday morning. Funny little memories, like a stupid TV commercial that he and Tommy would get a kick out of every time they saw it. He recalled how he and the teenager who had become like a son would recite and imitate the spoof; laughing at their own antics until their heads hurt. Random, seemingly innocuous things that ushered in waves of memories and the emotions that rode them.

"Whoever said love is stronger than death? Hats off to you, Sir, because you surely knew what you were talking about," mutters Charles to himself as he guns through his closet in search of a comfortable shirt to put on for tonight's "Boys Night Out" in Manhattan. Satisfied with what he sees in the mirror, despite his dissatisfaction with what's going on in his heart; the tall, dark, jean clad man leaves the solitude of his bedroom; grabs his keys, steps out into the night and into his waiting vehicle and heads east toward the brighter city lights just a few miles ahead.

Weaving his tall muscular body through the noisy sports bar crowd; Charles finally spots the guys seated around a rather large circular wooden table sans table cloth spilling over with an array of beverages, chips, pretzels, nachos and half-eaten burgers and fries.

"Finally, my man. You made it!" shouts Ty over the ruckus of laughing, shouting and loud talking men that fill the popular spot to capacity. Charles seats himself between Carlos and Eddie and across from Ty who just reached over the mountain of food and beverages to greet him.

"We were wondering what happened to you, man. How ya' doing?" adds Carlos, patting Charles on the back as he adjusts himself in his seat.

"Good, man. How are you?" responds Charles avoiding Carlos' direct stare and assessment of his countenance.

"Man, sorry about you and Dee's split up." Offers Carlos with genuine concern and compassion.

"Yeah, thanks, man. I appreciate it. I'll be alright."

"You see, this is what I'm talking about!" Ty barges his way into the dialog uninvited. "How'z a Black woman in America breaking up with a brotha' with a job, a house, a car, goes to church and actually believes what the preacher is saying and gotta' prayer life too?" Ty pauses for effect and then continues.

"Man, if I weren't a dude I'd try to marry you myself!" he finishes momentarily breaking the crowd up in laughter. "I told ya' to leave that one alone, son. But you just wouldn't listen!"

"How about Cindy's friend Tina?" chimes in Carlos. "She'd be great for my man!"

"Nah, that wouldn't work," interjects Eddie.
Looking furtively at Ty, he adds, "for the obvious reasons."
Ignoring Eddie's innuendo, Ty continues in agreement with Carlos.

"Yeah, besides she's a little closer to your age. Dee was too old for you, man. I told you that too, Professor!" Ty continues his harangue while dipping a nacho chip into sour cream and stuffing it into his open mouth.

"Is all of this sage advice suppose to make me feel better?" states Charles looking around the table unable to shroud his annoyance and irritation.

"Uh, oh. Professor is pulling out the $100 dollar words; think we've got him mad!" Jokingly states Ty testing the limits.

"Waiter, tab please."

"Whoa, my man! Why are you leavin'? You just got here?" Asks Ty.

"Because if I don't leave, I'll lose my religion."

"Ok, buddy! We'll stop." Sincerely offers Ty.

"Just trying to cheer you up, man, that's all. We actually planned this get together for your sake," finishes Ty.

"Yeah, we're just trying to take your mind off of Dee. Help you move on, man," Carlos chimes in again.

"Look man, Priscilla and I separated for 6 months about 3 years ago. It was the worse 6 months of my life." Offers Ed.

"I feel you, man. Losing a woman that you truly love kills something inside of you," adds Carlos.

"Yeah, remember when I broke up with Lucille back in 2000? Ty adds.

"How could I forget? You landed on my doorstep at 3 am in the morning?" quips Charles. Light laughter breaks the tension around the table. Ty continues,

"Yeah, man. I seriously felt like I was on the backside of never. It was like being drop kicked into a pit with no hope of getting rescued."

"That's impressive." Says Eddie smiling at Ty.

"What?" Ty questions with mock annoyance.

"Your poetic reflection on the experience." Chuckles Eddie.

"Didn't know that you had it in you." Eddie sarcastically adds tipping his empty glass and capturing a couple of ice cubes in his mouth for emphasis. Ty waves Ed's comments away and turns his attention back to Charles who rises to leave despite the protest of the men around the table.

"Thanks, but it's late and I have a paper due on Monday," states Charles opening his wallet and placing two crisp 20 dollar bills on the table.

"Ok, Professor," concedes Ty. "We'll catch up with you later. Feel better, man." Ty sincerely offers as he also rises to give Charles a man hug. The others around the table follow suit; releasing Charles into a sea of boisterous men as he once again navigates his way through the crowded restaurant-bar toward the exit. He then seems to disappear beyond the entrance no longer in sight and into the cool of the night.

Once outside, Charles checks his phone for the time noting that the hour is now past midnight. Although it's been months since he and Deirdre parted ways; he finds himself secretly hoping to see a familiar number in his message inbox; but doesn't. Wishful thinking. Charles releases an involuntary groan that only he can hear and feel. It's an internal longing that beer, nachos and a burger with the guys at a sports bar on a Friday night can not fulfill.

Heart break.

Man size.

It doesn't get analyzed with friends; talked-out and never openly cried-out. After all, strong men don't cry; especially over a woman. "Or '*the woman*' ; the one and only woman for me," Charles quietly interjects, interrupting his own thoughts.

The walk from the bar to the parking garage was only a block and a half away; but felt like an eternity. Seemed that every woman Charles passed on the street in some way reminded him of Dee. He felt weak. Vulnerable. Stupid. Angry. Finally reaching his car; he tips the attendant, gets in and drives back across the bridge and home to New Jersey not feeling any better than he did when he left nearly an hour and a half ago.

"If not us, then who?" --Rick J. Spratt, Jr.

Work was a great escape for Charles. Both his physical labor by day and his academic work by night were safe harbors for his restlessness. Work was a pain neutralizer-- didn't make it disappear altogether, but it did push it into the background, at least for little chunks of time. The only problem was when all of the activity stopped, the full-force of his heartache began, all over again.

When he was younger, he chose to solve the problem with a late night call to one of the many willing women who with hopes of a more permanent union would gladly answer his call. Sexual healing? Perhaps. He thought it safer and more pleasurable than the other drug induced highs. At least with the sexual Rx; the only apparent hang-over was getting rid of his overnight guest in the morning.

The use of women, drugs, alcohol and even work to assuage his emotional pain seemed to work for him in his 20's; but as a 38 year old man looking 40 square in the face; somehow it simply no longer satisfied. "When I was a child, I spoke as a child, I understood as a child, I thought as a child; but when I became a man, I put away childish things," Charles whispered to himself as he completed his on-line registration for his final 6 credit hours to at last finish his bachelors degree in History and English.

Just as he was about to stroke the final keys to close his application, he receives an AIM message from his former Heritage roommate who now serves as Dean of Continuing Education and Adult Studies at the college.

"Hey man, tried to reach you on your cell phone last week, but you were out of pocket. Need to talk to you about something. It's urgent. Call me. TONIGHT!!!"

"OK."

Charles simply typed in response feeling no need to get into the usual repartee with his old roommate. Clicking off AIM to avoid any further interruptions, Charles continued his registration, his last courses for earning his bachelors degree, he hopes.

An hour or so later…

"Hey man, how is it going?" Rick asks in his usual exuberance. Richard J. Spratt, Jr. was probably the most hyper upbeat man that Charles had ever encountered in his life. He simply didn't know anyone like Rick. The guy literally bounced off the walls with energy and excitement. He was one of those people who seemed happy just to be alive. His enthusiasm was contagious, but one really had to prepare to engage in even a brief conversation with Rick because his mouth and his mind moved at the speed of light.

"Listen man, I got approval on a program that I've been working on for more than a minute. It's for adult learners, particularly Heritage alumni who had their college or university educations interrupted at some point for reasons beyond their control.

I was actually thinking about you man when putting this thing together." He pauses briefly and continues, " How you had to leave your dream of a Heritage degree to take care of your mom. Never forgot the day that you packed up half of our dorm room and said good-bye, man. I remember thinking how much of a man you were to make such a sacrifice and wondered if I could ever do something like that.

You were so close to finishing, man," Rick adds reflectively. There was a silent pause before the words of the speaking man settled. He continued, "Anyway, like I was saying folks like you who were more than half-way through their degree program will be allowed to not only finish their bachelors but also earn a Master's Degree in an accelerated one-year program."

"You mean I can transfer these on-line credits back to Heritage, take my last 6 credit hours on-line with Heritage and still get my Heritage degree?"

"Yes, Sir!"

"Sounds almost too good to be true."

"Well, it is true. The only thing is that you have to relocate for the year to complete the program on campus."

"What? Man, I can't do that! I have a home and a job that I've been on for 20 years. Not to mention a woman who I intend to make my wife and her teenage son, my son. How am I going to drop everything and move to Atlanta for a year? That's crazy!"

"Do you want the degrees?" Rick questions. "You're finishing your bachelors with the Heritage name as if though you never left the college. Plus! You're earning an MBA or Masters of Arts in a year, man! You can't beat that with a stick, Son!" Rick pauses.

"Look man, you're a perfect candidate for this program. You're exactly the profile and demographic that we're seeking. Besides you'll make me look good if I pull a Heritage Man back into the fold!" Rick chuckles briefly. Shifting back to a more serious note, he adds,

"Times are tough man, the college has a solid endowment, but we're still in need of new revenue sources. Yes, I am doing this for brothers like you, man. But largely, I'm doing it for 'The House'. Can't stand to see another cut back in curriculum and student services due to financial restraints. We must keep the school solvent and prospering," he concludes adding,

"If not us, then who?"

Charles thanks his buddy and bids him farewell promising to think about his offer and get back to him on it. Reclining in his chair, he stretches his arms above his head and then rests them comfortably behind his head; smiling for the first time in a very long time.

"Only, God," he says aloud to himself as he moves to shut everything down and off for the night and go to bed. Moments later, just as he kneels bedside to thank his personal 'Miracle Maker,' his phone indicates that he just received a text message.

"Really miss you. Really sorry. Please forgive me. Dee."

"No, I will not forgive you." Charles replies.

"Unless you agree to marry me." He adds afterwards in an intentionally delayed response.

"Really??? Are you serious, Charles? Did you just propose to me via text?" Deirdre immediately shoots back with enough ire to penetrate any cloud in cyberspace. Charles ignoring both her text response and the numerous attempts that she makes to call him says a quick but heartfelt *"Thank you, Father"* heavenward rising from his kneeling position. In one fluid movement he grabs the black velvet box that he has had stashed in his nightstand drawer for months; throws on a discarded shirt and pair of jeans and heads out of his house at 2 am in the morning to claim his soon to be 'better half.'

As if expecting his arrival, Dee opens the door on the first ring and rushes into Charles' arms with a sense of urgency that is only surpassed by his own. The forlorn lovers tumble into an eternal moment where time and space stand still.

"I love you, Dee," whispers Charles releasing her just long enough to capture her mouth in full once again. He continues, stopping himself again.

"I really want us to spend the rest of our lives together. Dee, please be my wife." He pleads. Pausing to take in her every breath, he continues,

"I need you as much as I want you, baby." Charles says now looking directly into the tearing doe-eyed woman's very soul. Dropping to one knee; he pulls the black velvet box from the recesses of his pocket and presents a brilliant jewel.

"Oh, My God, Charles!"

"Please say yes, Dee."

"Oh, my goodness! I don't believe this is happening!" Exclaims Deirdre in a considerable degree of arousal, shock and excitement. The unexpected mix of emotions is explosive; simply leaving her speechless and in tears.

"Success and failure are equally a culmination of a series of personal choices, Son."   *--Uncle Pete*

3 months later…

Charles managed to put off telling Dee about Rick's offer to finish his degree at Heritage. With wedding plans underway; there never seemed to be a right time to break the news. However, Rick was now pressuring him for an answer on the weekly basis. Charles hesitantly picked up his phone. "Dee" he speaks into the device, using the few seconds saved in using the voice activated auto-dial to gather his feral thoughts.

"Hi, Sweetie," answers Dee cheerfully.

"What's up?" she questions.

"Hey, baby. Nothing much. Can you stop by some time this weekend when you get a chance?" Charles asks.

"Sure, Charles. What's up?" she asks a second time. "You sound a little stressed." Says Dee with genuine concern.

"Ah, nothing, baby. Just have a lot on my mind."

"Ok, Charles." Dee responds, not fully convinced that she's getting the full story. "I'll stop-by some time tomorrow."

"Oh, don't forget, we have an appointment on Monday evening with the caterer in New York." Deirdre reminds Charles.

"I won't forget." Charles responds. "Love you, baby. Good night."

"Me too," offers Deirdre as they both release their respective lines and return to their evening activities. Charles to his relentless mental wrestling; and Deirdre to her musings over their impending nuptials. She pours over a stack of bridal magazines chuckling to herself. The woman who promised that she would never marry again; was now preparing to do just that! "Never, say never," she reminds herself smiling as she circles yet another potential wedding gown idea before turning off her bedside lamp for the night and embracing all of the warm feelings that are floating around at the very center of her being.

"Knock, knock," Deirdre sings into the kitchen door as she lets herself into Charles' house.

"Hey, baby." Charles says rising up from the breakfast nook table to give Deirdre a quick but affectionate peck on the cheek.

"Hey yourself!" she smiles grabbing a plump seedless grape from the top of an unpacked grocery bag sitting idly on the kitchen counter. "You're up and about early this Saturday morning? Where's Tommy," asks Charles now leaning against the kitchen countertop next to Deirdre, arms folded and relaxed.

"Basketball. He's in a tournament in Rockland County all day. I am going up at noon. Wanna go?" asks Deirdre rinsing another grape grabbed from the bag and popping it into her mouth.

"Hmmmm, these are good. So, sweet!"

"Umhmm, just like you." Charles offers as he gently reaches over and pulls Deirdre toward him, planting a kiss on her grape-filled mouth.

"Hmmmm. That is good," he whispers.

"Umhmm," responds Deirdre.

"Tastes like some more," says Charles as he kisses Deirdre again, this time more deeply.

"OK, Sir". Deirdre playfully announces. "You're about to jeopardize your promise!" Warns Deirdre as she wiggles herself free from his embrace and pulls back just enough to look into Charles' eyes. Charles chuckles.

"Yeah, you're right. Let me stop, before I can't." Charles admits.

"Lord, give me strength," he resolutely sighs.

"Thanks!"

"Oh, don't thank me," teases Deirdre.

"I am just trying to help a brotha' out," she laughs moving toward the frig to continue her snacking.

"So, what's up? You said that you needed to talk to me about something? " Deirdre inquires while quickly scanning the contents of Charles' half-full refrigerator.

"Yeah, there is something that I need to discuss with you." Charles responds slowly while taking the rest of the groceries out of the bag and handing them to Deirdre to put in the frig.
"Got a call from Rick not too long ago," Charles momentarily pauses. "You remember me telling you about my friend Rick? My college roomie from Heritage?"

"Yes, you introduced us over the phone when we first started dating." Deirdre reminds him.

"I did?" questions Charles with an incredulous furrow of his brow.

"Yep. You sure did."

"Wow!"

"Wow, what?" Deirdre asks moving toward the breakfast nook to sit down with a bowl of granola and a cup of yogurt.

"Just surprised how quickly things have happened between us."

"Well, not all things…" suggests Deirdre with a smirk. Charles looks at Deirdre intently for a moment and just shakes his head.

"Woman, you need Jesus."

"Got him." Quips Deirdre. "Just don't have him to the extent that you do. I've also learned the hard way not to make promises to God that I can't keep," Deirdre flippantly continues while scooping the last spoon of yogurt into her mouth.

"Whatever, Deirdre." Says Charles turning the playful banter somewhat serious. Staying with the sudden change in the tone of their conversation, Deirdre asks,

"So , what is it that you wanted to talk to me be about?"

"Oh, right. Like I was saying, my buddy Rick runs the Continuing Ed and Adult Studies at Heritage and recently started a program to get former Heritage brothers like me who for whatever reason could not complete our degrees to finish our programs."

"That's awesome, Charles! But aren't you almost finished?"

"6 hours left."

"So what would be the sense in enrolling in the Heritage program if you're almost finished on-line?" asks Deirdre with a note of concern as she now divides her attention with a supermarket circular on the table in front of her.

"Well, first of all, I would be getting the Heritage degree that I've always wanted. In fact, successful completion of the program awards both a bachelor and master's degree in Liberal Arts or Business in less than two years."

"Really?" Deirdre asks incredulously.

"Really." Charles replies while moving a wayward strand of hair from in front of her eyes.

"Then go for it Professor!"
Deirdre playfully shouts clapping her hands like a happy little girl.

"You're so crazy!"

"No, really Charles, it sounds like a wonderful opportunity and the answer to your prayers."

"Well not all of them, Dee." Charles adds growing momentarily silent.

"Why? Charles, what's wrong?"

"Nothing is wrong, it's just that the program requires that candidates live on or near campus."

"In Atlanta, Charles?" inquires Dee with a note of anxiety.

"Dee, you're acting like Georgia is the end of the earth. It's a somewhat short flight, not a big deal." Charles offers attempting to reassure. He continues, "I can get home at least once a month."

"I see that you already have all of this planned out, Charles?" Dee says exasperated.

"What about us? Did you forget that we're planning a wedding, Charles!" says Dee unable to control a flood of emotion.

"What about the three of us? What am I going to tell Tommy? Who will be here for him? Who is going to be here for me Charles if you leave?" Dee says on the brink of tears.

"Deirdre, I am not going anywhere! I mean, yes, I am leaving physically, but I am not leaving the relationship emotionally or spiritually, or physically... Lord, what am I saying?" says Charles feeling trapped in the middle of something he can't comfortably get out of.

"I don't know Charles, because what I am hearing is that you're leaving for a whole year or possibly even two to live in Atlanta to finish your degree," Dee says unable to hold back the moisture teeming at the rims of her eyelids. She continues,

"And what I'm not hearing is what all of this is going to mean for Tommy and I!" laments Deirdre with tears now flowing freely. In effort to comfort, Charles gently rises from the opposite side of the table and moves around the nook to share the bench on the other side with Deirdre.

"Baby look, this is my dream and it is one that I have been laboring in for nearly two decades." Says Charles putting his arm around Dee's quivering shoulder and drawing her nearer. Without resistance Dee sighs turning her body into Charles' and rests her head on his waiting shoulder. Wiping her own tears slowly, she speaks calmly for the first time in a few minutes.

"So, what does all of this mean?" She sighs a second time.

"What is going to happen to us?" Dee asks adjusting herself so that she is eye to eye with Charles.

"Well, my love, what it means is that you and Tommy have a new home…"

"Charles, I am not moving to Atlanta!"

"Woman, let me finish… As I was saying, You and Tommy can move in here while I am away…"

"Charles, if I could afford to carry a mortgage I would already own my own home," says Dee cutting Charles off a second time.

"Lord, woman! Can a man get a word in edgewise? Let me talk, baby!"

"Ok, Ok. I'm sorry." Dee confesses. "I'll stop talking and listen."

"Thank you," says Charles shaking his head as he attempts for a third time to explain his plan for them.

"Ok. Your lease is up in September and the owner wants to sell; which means you need a new place for you and Tommy. We're getting married sometime next year; we're going to live here at least until Tommy graduates from high school. So, why not just move in while I'm away?" concludes Charles.

"Because it simply doesn't feel right, Charles." States Deirdre matter-of-factly.

"What do you mean, it doesn't feel right?" Implores Charles. "We are engaged to be married in less than a year; you are about to be my wife. What could possibly be wrong with us beginning the process of merging our lives on a practical and financial level, Dee?" Questions Charles without waiting for an answer.

"I don't understand what the problem is," he continues noting Dee's resistance. Dee shifts uncomfortably under his gaze, not wanting to give in.

"I think you're just being headstrong and stubborn." Succinctly concludes Charles.

"I'm not." Resolutely declares Deirdre with arms now folded defiantly across her chest.

"Yeah, you are, girl."

"You're as stubborn as a country mule."

"I am not, Charles."

"Then tell me why, Dee?"

"You need the space and the time to financially regroup, yet you flatly reject my offer to help you." Charles pauses, then adds,

"You're hurting me, baby."

"How am I hurting you Charles by refusing to move into your house with my teenage son before we are married?" Questions Dee. "If anything, I'm helping you; if you know what I mean?"

"Oh woman, please." Charles responds exasperated. "You don't have to move in until I leave for Atlanta." The mention of his imminent departure elicits a fresh stream of tears down Deirdre's now tranquil face.

"Oh, baby. Don't start crying again." Charles pleads drawing her close and gently wiping her tears away with his hand.

"Look, you and I both know the real reason why the idea of you living here while I'm away bothers you."

"Oh really, Mr. Know it All? And what is the reason, Charles?" Queries Deirdre recovering from the last bout of tears enough to re-engage Charles in their debate.

"You're afraid of feeling too dependent on me, Dee."

"I am not."

"Yeah, Dee. You are."

"You think you know everything, don't you?"

"Nope, but I know you, my lady." Charles smiles gently as he lifts her chin and plants a kiss on the tip of her nose. Dee releases a sigh of resignation as he rises to leave the table and finish putting the last of the groceries away.

"Dee, we are about to become one. You, Tommy and I are about to be a family. We're suppose to depend on each other; be there for one another; no matter what." Charles finishes, adding, "That's what real family is about," as he puts the final grocery item in the frig.

"May I please have some of that water before you put it away?" asks Dee somewhat wearily.

"I'm thirsty."

"Every blessing comes with responsibility and a good measure of sacrifice."

--Rev. Elijah Mordecai Smith

Much to Charles' chagrin; but not at all to his surprise, Deirdre held her ground on not moving into his house for the year or so while he was away. As much as he wanted the opportunity to bring a life long dream into fruition; it was not an easy price to pay. Leaving Dee and Tommy behind was emotionally expensive and something that he could only fully admit to himself and God. The promised monthly returns home were kept; but just made his being away that much harder on everyone.

Wedding plans, however chugged right along without as much as a hiccup. Appointments were kept with florists, bridal consultants, couture seamstresses, tuxedo rental shops and banquet houses on each of Charles' return trips home and often by Dee, solo in his absence. Technology allowed Charles to virtually be in on any wedding-related meeting or conversation necessary. But no amount of virtual presence soothed Dee's need to be in Charles' physical presence on the regular basis. Oddly enough, even before Charles moved to Atlanta, they weren't a couple that necessarily had to see each other everyday of the week. They had busy separate lives that for the most part satisfied them. Even when Charles was at home, they could go days without actually seeing each other as long as some type of communication between them was maintained either by phone, text or e-mail. But this was different. He was over 800 miles away; not across town.

Dee, as hard as she tried to stay positive about the situation, simply never adjusted to the idea of Charles being away and would too often find herself on an emotional roller coaster from week to week. Plain old-fashioned grumpiness over his absence would settle in on her as quickly as the joy of his return trips home. Busyness helped her cope to some degree, filling her days with the normal parenting duties and pleasures. However, Tommy was also no happy camper. Dee oft wondered who missed Charles more; her or her son. Nevertheless, Tommy, work and wedding planning occupied her time, energy and attention most days; leaving her alone to struggle with the unoccupied lonely hours of the night.

"Tommy! Let's go!" calls Deirdre from the next room attempting to move the teen from the snails pace mode that he always defaulted to when he didn't want to do something. "I want to get over to Charles' house and get some things done before he comes home next weekend."

"Awwh, Ma. Do I have to go this time?" The teenager whines. "I don't like being at Charles' house when he's not there," he continues. "It's no fun." Deirdre stops her rushing around her bedroom for a brief moment taking in her son's words and agrees. "He's right. This isn't fun," she says audibly to herself.

"Ok, Tommy. You can stay here. I'll only be a couple of hours." Deirdre concedes. "Please be ready for your basketball practice when I get back. I don't want to have to wait around all afternoon for you to get yourself together," Dee says as she grabs her car keys to leave. "And straighten up that room. It looks like a hurricane blew through there, boy!" She adds.

"Ok, Ma. See ya' when ya' get back," says the teen waving briefly to his departing mother without breaking the rhythm of his dancing thumbs gliding across the ever-present game system controller.

"Tommy, shut that thing off and get your room cleaned." Deirdre yells back up to the teen as she opens the front door to exit the house. "I'll be back before noon. If that room isn't clean when I get back, there will be no basketball today," Deirdre warns just before stepping over the threshold and out into a clear bright morning.

Dee made regular visits to Charles' house, despite the fact that she refused to move in while he was away. She still had keys and full access to everything that belonged to him. It was the concession made between her and Charles that she and Tommy would at least use the house while he was away. Tommy played games on the large screen, Dee did her laundry, dusted, opened mail and even wrote checks which Charles left behind for bills that he could not pay online. Sometimes she would fall asleep on the couch in the Family Room with Charles' favorite Jazz CD playing to keep her company. More than once, as if though sensing that she was there; Charles would call and indeed find her at the house in their favorite spot. Those conversations would always end with him smiling and shaking his head as he hung up the phone. "My soon to be *Mrs. Monroe*. What exactly am I going to do with you?" He would chuckle to himself returning to the mountain of books and multiple piles of paper in front of him.

"A garden enclosed is my sister, my spouse, a spring shut up, a fountain sealed." -- Song of Solomon

Sitting at his desk with only the light of his trusty laptop and a small desk lamp; Charles ponders the events of the last year and six months. A whirlwind romance. Love found, love lost and love reclaimed. Literally. He was within months of making Dee his wife and finishing the first phase of the Heritage Dual Degree Program. In just 2 months shy of his 40th birthday he would walk to the thunderous sound of the Heritage Marching Band's rendition of Pomp and Circumstance; and 6 months later walk down the sacred aisle of Mt. Moriah at Christmas time to exchange wedding vows with his beloved, Deirdre. It's was already early spring; the year seemed to have evaporated. With the monthly commute home to New Jersey, phone calls, text messages and e-mails; the distance seemed to strengthen and not weaken the soul-tie between Charles and Deirdre.

"Hey, baby. Did I wake you?" asks Charles making a late good night call home.

"Hi Sweetie. No, I am up reading."

"When are you coming home?" Deirdre immediately asks like an expectant child.

"I'm not sure if I am going to make it back this weekend." Apologetically states Charles anticipating Dee's reaction.

He continues, " I need to meet with my academic advisor first thing Monday morning to get my bachelor degree clearance paperwork done and chart out the remainder of the program." Charles finishes feeling the weight of Deirdre's disappointment.

"Deirdre?"

"Yes." She answers after a long pause of silence.

"Sweetheart we will have at least 3 or 4 weeks together in June for the summer," offers Charles lightly tapping his pen on his desk as he measures his words carefully. "I don't have to return until mid July to finish my practicum," he adds in attempt to console the brooding woman on the other end of the line.

"This is what I don't understand, Charles." Deirdre says unable to veil her irritation. "You have 20 years of practical work experience , 10 of which you've held supervisory roles here in New Jersey with the local Department of Sanitation and Public Works. Why in the world do you have to do a practicum at all?" Dee questions with unbridled frustration. "And at the Department of Public works in Atlanta, for goodness sake?" Complains Deirdre.

"Baby, you know that I tried to get the program director to give me credit for my work experience or at least allow me to do the practicum in New Jersey — but they said that "going-home" to do the practicum would not broaden or expand my perspective or the depth of my professional skill set ," Charles explains. "Look honey, it's only another six month's after our wedding and we're done. We're getting married Christmas." He reminds her.

"After our Honeymoon, I'll come back to Atlanta to finish the last phase of the program and then come home to my beautiful new wife for good; with an MBA in my hand and you in my arms." Charles reassures Dee and continues, "And as long as I've been waiting for you, I just hope that I can even make it back to finish the program after Christmas." Charles suggestively adds.

"Hmmmmm. Mr. Monroe, sounds to me like you have some business to handle and a plan for getting it done, Sir." Deirdre teases purposely choosing to shift away from her moodiness to a lighter spirit for Charles' sake. Charles noting Dee's change in disposition smiles to himself and continues the flirtation.

"So, were we able to book that villa in Negril for our Honeymoon?"

"Yep! We are getting a special Honeymoon Suite right on the beach with a private outdoor Jacuzzi; wet bar and a few other things that I will surprise you with on our Wedding Night." Deirdre chuckles seductively.

"Baby, there's only one thing I need you to do for me on our Wedding Night…"

"Charles!" Dee laughs feigning shock. "You need to stop!"

"That's exactly what I am planning not to do, young lady." Charles teases. "I am going to love you forever in and out of our marriage bed; like my very life depended on it, Dee." Charles gently proclaims instantly shifting the tone and intensity of their conversation. Dee takes pause again for a second time over the phone; but this time for a totally different reason.

"A generous man will prosper; he who refreshes others will himself be refreshed." -- Proverbs

Autumn... 3½ months before the Wedding

With the monthly commuting back and forth between New Jersey and Atlanta, tuition, the studio apartment he rented for the year, wedding and honeymoon costs, and all of the normal reoccurring monthly expenses at home: mortgage, *(no car note; the car was paid off 2 years ago!)*, insurance, utilities, the cable bundle, etc.; finances were getting tighter than Charles was accustomed to and comfortable with them being. Well-trained in the old-fashioned edict of "living below one's means," he was a man use to cash flow; not deficit.

The Sanitation Department granted him an unpaid leave of absence to earn the MBA and even picked up part of the tuition costs as long as Charles agreed to come back to the DPW with his newly earned degrees. 20 years, a good reputation and repoire with both the brass, rank and file, coupled with a fresh MBA would be more than an asset to the local Public Works Department. Charles only saw it as yet another blessing from above. However, at the moment he was feeling more pressure than blessing. Looking at the monthly budget under the singular light of a bright harvest moon and his desk lamp, Charles pushes the calculator and spreadsheet away, closes his eyes and rests his throbbing forehead in the open palm of his free hand as if commanding stillness over the constant adding, subtracting and dividing going on inside of his head.

"Okay," he sighs out loud to the stillness of the warm southern night with only the sound of the large wooden ceiling fan rushing to meet the echo of his voice. "Something has to give. I'll be broke by the time all of this is over!" he confesses.

"Lord, what am I going to do?" Charles questions leaning back in his chair rubbing his temples as if the answers to his dilemma reside there. "Maybe we need to cut the wedding guest list in half?" Charles suggests to himself attempting to think things through to a solution. "Nawh, that would only get me an unhappy bride; and I'm really not trying to go there," he chuckles to himself thinking of Dee.

"If mama is happy, everybody is happy. If she isn't… Lord knows!" he smiles before his thoughts attempt to slip him back to the state of worriment that he languished in only moments ago.

"Lord make a way, Father. I am outta' bullets," he whispers as he drags the spreadsheet and calculator back in front of him; circles three key items for re-consideration tomorrow. Placing two sharpened pencils with well-worn erasers on top of the document; he clicks off the desk lamp and sits quietly in the darkness for a moment before rising to retire for the night.

3 days later…

It's early afternoon, after class. Charles enters his studio apartment which is actually about the size of the Family Room in his home in New Jersey. Having long ago made the adjustments to the smaller living space and all of the other sacrifices necessary to accomplishing his goals in Atlanta; he moves the few steps needed to get to his work area and drops a pile of mail on his desk next to a half completed statistics research paper. A slight groan escapes as he sees the physical reminder of his unresolved dilemma. Several unpaid bills, and an unfinished paper.

"Umph," he releases a second time as he walks away from the pile; goes to the frig, grabs a carton of orange juice, chugs it and tosses the empty carton in a near by cylinder trashcan. He then goes back to the waiting pile and begins sorting through the unopened mail.

"Bill. Bill. Another bill. Bill…" Charles utters as he moves through the day's postal delivery. "Ernest?" he says with a note of curiosity and surprise.

"I wonder what's up?" he questions aloud to himself. "I don't have time for one of his dinner parties." He says with a tinge of impatience. He continues, "And since when has he ever sent me a formal invite to anything?" Charles says as he opens the thin linen envelope. Instantly jolted by its contents; he immediately sits down in attempt to make sense of what he is reading. In a handwritten note in cursive writing much too perfect to come from the hand of any man; Ernest briefly wrote:

Charles

Consider this an early Graduation, Birthday, Christmas, Wedding Gift.

Regards
Ernest and Marva

P.S. I'm really proud of you, Cuz! Perhaps you'll consider joining the company when you finish the program? Harvard and Heritage MBA's! What a team, eh?

E.W.M.

Encl: Check #9577, Amt: $250,000.00

"He brought me to the banqueting house,
and his banner over me was love." -- *Song of Solomon*

Mt. Moriah basks in a glow that is unique to the Christmas holiday season. There is a peace that prevails throughout the waiting Sanctuary filled not with seekers at the moment; but a stillness that envelopes the beauty of the early winter morning. The historic ecclesiastical edifice has a bridal room which came as a complete surprise to Deirdre. It was something she would not have ever known, despite her many Sunday morning visits. Until she became a bride-to-be it was like a hidden little secret only known to the chosen.

The small inviting room was tucked away in the Narthex of the Church seemingly always awaiting its next lovely bride. Simply furnished; an oversized chair and matching paisley footstool regally occupy its center with a matching 8ft. Victorian mirror that stands like the palace guard directly under the translucent radiance of a 19th Century French brass chandelier. The vintage garment rack and aromatic bouquet of fresh flowers that permeate every corner of the room delicately add to the ambiance of sacredness present in the atmosphere.

"Best man, here! Miss Dee, you have 30 minutes before show time!" Ty announces with a series of rapid knocks from the other side of the large mahogany door. He waits a few seconds for a response before moving swiftly along the corridor to the Pastor's Study which serves as the bridegrooms' dressing area for the day.

"Thanks, Ty!" Janice responds on Deirdre's behalf as the stylist quickly unties the hairnet that holds about a dozen colossal curlers in place on top of the bride's head.

"Thanks, J.," quietly states Dee barely moving a muscle as the stylist rhythmically plucks the hair pins from her large rollers. Janice smiles warmly at her best friend and turns her attention back to the other stylist in the room who is putting finishing touches on a peachy-coral lipstick that she has selected for her expressly for the occasion.

"Oh, I am so loving this color on me!" raves Janice as the other three bridesmaids scurry around the room putting on pantyhose, earrings, eyelashes, lip gloss, etc., Deirdre sits calmly in the midst of the swirl of activity with her eyes closed gently taking in and releasing long deep breaths.

"Ok, Dee. You're picture perfect. Just need to touch-up your make-up." States Gabriel; a tall angular gentleman in an exquisitely cut Italian suit.

"Shandra, pass me that peachy-coral lipstick," he calls out to his assistant who is now working on the next bridesmaid. With a gentle tap on Deirdre's slender shoulder, Gabriel indicates that his masterpiece is completed and beckons Deirdre to take a look in the mirror. Deirdre slowly opens her eyes and assesses the beautiful image that stares back at her and smiles.

"Wow! Thanks, Gabriel! You did an awesome job," she says carefully removing a stray eyelash from underneath her perfectly painted eyes.

"You're an easy woman to make even more beautiful, Dee." Your hair and skin are in excellent condition. Makes my job that much easier," says the stylish stylist offering the bride much needed assistance in rising from her chair.

"Lord knows I try, Gabriel," Deirdre admits accepting both the compliment and the gentleman's proffered help.

"Wow!"

is all that Charles can clearly think and manage to articulate upon seeing Dee for the first time in her Wedding Gown moving down the center aisle of the Sanctuary toward him like an angel on a cloud. He drops his head momentarily in attempt to regain his composure. However, his efforts are short-lived when he raises his head again only to have Deirdre so quickly before him gazing up at him with a look of utter vulnerability that completely disarms him.

"You're beautiful." Charles silently mouths to Dee. Shyly she mouths back, *"Thank you,"* before they both turn their attention to Pastor Chuck who begins the ceremony with prayer.

"Lord, we are gathered here today to witness the joining of two hearts together as one; two souls joined in one purpose; two minds joined in one vision. Charles and Deirdre desire to reflect your idea of marriage through

their sacred union, here in this sacred place, in this sacred hour. Oh Lord, it is before You, their family, friends and loved ones that this man and woman will make their wedding vows. The vows that Charles and Deirdre will make before your altar today Lord are an earthly covenant that resonates in heaven because it reflects Your will, Your vision, Your glory and even Your relationship to mankind. We pray, Father God that Charles will love Deirdre like Christ loved the Church; and that Deirdre in turn will respect Charles. We ask that Peace, Joy and Love reign in their day-to-day marital relations; and that Patience, Self-Control and Faith under gird their home, family life and interactions with each other. Let Kindness, Goodness and Gentleness be their reasonable service unto each other. And let them not be conformed to this world, but be transformed daily by the renewing of their minds and their love for You and for each other. Holy Spirit, be with them; and keep them with You! Father, please hear our prayers today on behalf of this precious couple. It's in the glorious and matchless name of Jesus Christ, our Lord and our Savior that we ask these blessings upon this marriage. Amen."

Tears flow freely from the bride as well as the groom; and just about everyone else from the bridal party to the ushers royally positioned at the entrance of the Sanctuary. The vows and the gold bands that symbolize the most sacred earthly commitment made between a man and a woman are exchanged to the immense joy of all who are privileged to share and be witnesses of this uniquely special moment in time for Charles and Deirdre.

"You may kiss the bride," encourages the clergyman. Smiling like an angel from a place deep within her soul, Dee allows her newly wedded husband to lift her partial veil and seal their vows with a kiss.

Awake, O North wind and Come, O South!
Blow upon my garden, that its spices may flow out!
Let my beloved come to his garden and eat its pleasant fruits."
                                                    —Song of Solomon

Author's Notes, Historical References, End Notes Page

- All opening and closing chapter quotations are either direct quotes or references to the Holy Bible (KJV, NKJV, NIV).

- Heritage College is a fictional Historically Black College (HBC) based on the HBC's established in 1867 under the Freedman's Bureau Federal Reconstruction Act of 1865 following the end of the Civil War. The Freedman's Bureau was created to educate newly freed African American slaves during the Post Civil War Reconstruction Era.

- United Negro College Fund is a non-profit organization established in 1944 dedicated to national fundraising efforts to provide scholarships for social-economically underprivileged college-bound African American students. *"A mind is a terrible thing to waste"* is the organization's slogan.

- The Civil Rights Movement 1950 to 1968

- Montgomery Bus Strike 1958

- Memphis Sanitation Workers Strike 1968 Protest Slogan: *"I AM A MAN!" (Thanks! RFJ*)*

- The Great Depression (1929 to 1939)

- World War II (1941-1945)

- The Great Migration (1940's)